from

Merle Collins is Grenadian. She was a member of Grenada's National Women's Organisation until 1983. Her poetry has appeared in a number of anthologies, and her own collection, *Because the Dawn Breaks*, was published by Karia Press in 1985. She co-edited and contributed to *Watchers and Seekers: Creative Writing by Black Women in Britain* (The Women's Press, 1987), and is author of *Angel*, an outstanding first novel centred on the lives of three generations of Grenadian women (The Women's Press, 1987). She is currently a member of African Dawn, a group which performs dramatised poetry fused with African music.

Merle Collins

Rain Darling

Stories

The Women's Press

Published by the Women's Press Limited 1990
A member of the Namara Group
34 Great Sutton Street, London EC1V 0DX

British Library Cataloguing in Publication Data
Collins, Merle
    Rain darling
    I. Title
    813 [F]

ISBN 0-7043-4258-8

Typeset in 10pt Bembo by MC Typeset Limited,
Gillingham, Kent
Printed and bound in Great Britain by BPCC Hazell Books
Member of BPCC Ltd, Aylesbury, Bucks England

You carry my life
In the sadness of your eyes
In the anguish of your tears
In the silence of your fears

When you let them stop you walking
My step falters
When you let them stop you talking
My voice becomes weaker
When you let them stop you looking
My eyes grow dimmer
When you let them stop you reasoning
My thoughts become confused

If you think they might stop you
wanting to re-create
Look for the rest of us
You carry our lives
In the questions in your eyes
Just like we carry yours

Contents

Acknowledgments

My thanks for detailed comments on the early manuscript to Jacob Ross and Marva Buchanan, and to Rhonda Cobham-Sanders for her usual thorough editorial work. (For creole words used in this collection, see glossary on pages 183 and 184.)

Rain

The old stone walls of the building towered above the women as they walked up the hill. They walked slowly, stopping, turning, looking down at the city spread out beneath them. The land stretched like an open palm towards the sea. The blue waters licked the spaces between the outstretched fingers. Buildings looked like they should not have been there, postcard intrusions painted on by a fanciful artist. From where the women were watching, the houses were a mixture of green and red and orange and white and yellow colours, a raging argument painted on the face of peace. In the distance, the bright blue sky curved to kiss the sea. Paz was a beautiful city, its name the ironic gift of a lustful conqueror with a twisted sense of humour.

Sister drew a deep and audible breath, pursed her lips and breathed out into the sunshine.

'Somebody down there pushing fire, yes!' she looked down towards Paz, wiping her brow. Took off the wide-brimmed straw hat, stood with one arm akimbo, her mouth half-opened, fanning her face and drinking in the coolness of the temporary breeze.

Ermintrude turned, watched her cousin, put her own hand to her head, but dropped it without removing the soft blue felt hat. She, too, looked down at the outstretched right hand of Paz.

The three women walked, each lost in thought. Unable to keep up the pace, Ermintrude gradually fell back. Usually, she was a good walker, but the sun burned through the felt hat and sent rivulets of sweat down the side of her face, stiffened her legs and prevented rapid progress. The long-sleeved polyester blouse clung to her body. Ermintrude put up her hand and removed the hat after all.

Sister looked back just in time to see the action. She had told her; she had warned her cousin that those clothes, that blouse and that long thick skirt, would make her steam in the heat. But these people who stay for such a long time in the cold in America always want to wear all kind of long-sleeve when they come on holiday! But Ermintrude should know better! She must be steaming! Not too far now, anyway. And she must be worried about seeing Rain, too. That was another problem.

Sister was thinking about the two bags that she had given to the bus driver that morning. Sometimes on these Sunday trips the drivers were so crazy! She just hoped that he had given them to her cousin, Nurse Jones, as she had requested. It should be all right; that particular driver was their cousin, too; distant, but a relation. If he hadn't done it, they would have had to visit Rain empty-handed; everyone had packed their things in those bags; empty-handed except for the little rice and peas and chicken she was carrying in that bag slung over her shoulder, and whatever little Ermintrude had kept to carry in her own little bag. Sister wondered what Ermintrude would give to her sister at the hospital. Rain didn't like her too much! Rain didn't like anybody too much! Except Cousin Lyris, of course. Poor Rain! She had had a hard life, though! Sister realised that she was thinking about her cousin in the past tense.

'Well!' She said the word out loud, fanning her face against the heat.

Cousin Lyris glanced back at Sister, wondering what she was thinking. She was surprised that Sister had decided to make the afternoon trip with them. She must know that Rain wouldn't want to see her. They hadn't treated her well! Poor girl! Hers was a hard, hard, life! A hard life! People not supposed to have to go through that kind of thing! She wondered how Ermintrude was feeling about this visit. She hadn't said much, but in a way it would have been better for her to go alone. The sisters would need some time to talk. If Rain would talk! Still, Ermintrude had wanted them to accompany her. She must tell the others that they should leave the sisters alone for a while. She thought about the bags that Sister had given to Moira's son, the bus driver. He was reliable. They should be all right. And a good thing she had done that, too. Imagine walking up this hill with those heavy bags! Ermintrude had shown her two really nice pairs of shoes that she had brought for Rain. And the inevitable grey dresses. Rain should like them. If she looked at them. She glanced back at the others criss-crossing up the hill to make the journey easier.

'Youall come on, come on! We almost there, now! I twice you age, and you letting me beat allyou like that?'

'I don't know where you does get you energy from, non. It must be in the height. You twice my height, too.'

'Well you self, Ermintrude, you have no height at all, so don't talk! At least I in the middle, but you, you nowhere near cousin Lyris!'

'True, yes,' agreed Ermintrude. 'Cousin Lyris height don't come from the Augier side of the family at all! Mother and Aunt Myra and all of them is a short, short set of people. That must be come from her father people! She like Rain! Is that kind of height.'

The conversation paused abruptly, the women pushed back into thought. No-one commented. Oh dear! thought Cousin Lyris! The unmentionable! And it just wasn't right! It was all that damn man's fault! Her mother said so! She had brought up the subject with Ermintrude. Ermintrude had said, 'Well Aunt Myra is one person inside the family I hear that come out and give me mother right. And Aunt Emma say she don't know, but whatever she do is all right. She do it because she had a reason! And Orilie, I never talk to her about it, but you know what she will feel. I don't like to talk about it at all!'

They went through the stone archway into the wide courtyard. A few people were standing around, talking. Some were obviously visitors, dressed in their Sunday best for the outing; some were patients. Two nurses leaned against the wall; one was looking through the porthole towards Paz and the sea. The other walked towards them. Cousin Lyris thought, She really better go alone first!

'Listen,' she said, 'Ermintrude, I think is best if you go in to see her alone, and then we will come afterwards.'

'But . . .' Both Ermintrude and Sister were protesting.

Sister was thinking, I sure Cousin Lyris and Ermintrude plan this! But then Ermintrude seemed genuinely surprised, so perhaps not. Why should Cousin Lyris take it upon herself to suggest such a thing? She, Sister, wasn't afraid to face Rain. There was no *reason* why she should keep away from Rain.

Ermintrude was strangely afraid of facing her sister alone. She didn't want to see the rejection, the resentment on her face. But perhaps Cousin Lyris was right. It was better to face it alone, especially not with Sister. Perhaps it was a good idea after all! Let her sort out things with her sister first! If Rain would let anybody sort things out with her!

'Okay, then.' Ermintrude turned towards the nurse, and Sister shrugged her shoulders.

Cousin Lyris walked towards one of the portholes. Sister moved to one of the benches in the courtyard. From the porthole, where in olden times the guns of the fort used to scan the sea, Cousin Lyris could see both sides of the cross. Only one side of Paz had been visible as they walked up the hill, one hand stretching out into the sea. Now, from this building at the top of the hill, the frightening beauty of Paz City was all spread out below. From here it was obvious why the Spanish tourists called it Cruz. In the middle, one stretch of land jutted right out into the sea. On it was a large building, with a red roof and grey walls, the old leper house. On the way up they had seen one hand; now the other hand stretched to Cousin Lyris' right, fingers spread. Paz! Crucified and beautiful in the sunshine.

Cousin Lyris turned and looked towards the long, low, new brick building hiding behind these old stone walls of the ancient fort. On the verandah, she could see Ermintrude's felt hat, her left arm on the verandah railing, her face in profile as she talked to the person sitting behind the post, out of sight. Rain, she guessed. Cousin Lyris walked to the bench and sat with Sister.

People said this place up here was haunted. There were all sorts of stories about how in the night the soldiers could be heard moving around in search of parts of their bodies, looking for fingers, and ears, and feet. Some said that sometimes on a moonlit night, people could see just a head moving, looking for the rest. Or just a foot moving, looking for the rest. But the worst were the souls which had lost whole bodies, and you heard them when the wind was howling and howling and howling through the mouth of the guns pointing down to Paz.

Cousin Lyris shivered. The wind was cold in this place. There were some things you shouldn't think about even in broad daylight with the sun shining on you.

When Ermintrude came out to call them, they were just sitting there, saying nothing, lost in thought. Sister pushed herself to her feet.

'How is she?'

Ermintrude shrugged. 'She all right. Come, non.'

Rain was standing at the verandah railing, tall and slim. Her shoulders were held straight. She was stately and assured when you saw her from afar, a thick black plait circling her head. She became smaller, somehow, when you tried to look into her eyes. Perhaps she knew this, and so she usually tried to avoid meeting anyone's eyes. Unless she wanted to, and then she sometimes had such an intense stare that you felt uncomfortable.

'Rain, how are you?'

Rain stared at Sister. 'Why you want to know how I am? Why you come here? Youall have no shame, you and your mother? She send you to finish me off?' Rain's voice was quiet, conversational. Her liquid black eyes never left Sister's face.

Sister laughed nervously. 'Don't excite yourself, Rain. You know the doctor say you mustn't take things on.'

Rain gave a twist of a smile. 'I not excited, Cousin. I have nothing to be excited about.'

'Your Auntie Orilie dead, Rain. She can't send nobody to finish you off,' Cousin Lyris said, smiling.

'I know she dead, Cousin Lyris. Don't let them make you think I mad; I have me full senses.'

'Yes,' said Cousin Lyris quietly. 'Yes, yes, all right'.

'Don't all right me. I not stupid. These people who so wicked in life don't really die, you know. They keep contact with those they want to carry out their deeds here.' Rain looked at Sister, and backed away a step. 'They don't really die.'

Sister looked at Ermintrude, smiled, put a finger to her temple, and shook her head. Rain looked at her sister. Ermintrude lifted her shoulders as if to say, What to do! Rain said quietly, 'I think I better go inside and lie down.'

Cousin Lyris drew Sister aside. 'You know how it is,' she said, 'I think you better wait outside.'

Sister sucked her teeth. 'But why she behaving like that?'

Cousin Lyris said again, 'You know how it is,' and inwardly asked Rain to forgive her for pretending.

Sister walked down the steps. Rain watched her go, watched her turn left and disappear within the courtyard. She turned back to look at her sister and cousin, then moved to sit on a chair. The two women walked towards the long bench.

'How are you feeling, Rain?'

Rain shrugged. 'So–so.' She stared out into the sunshine. After a moment, she added, 'Is just the cough, otherwise I'm all right.'

A nurse came forward with the bags that Ermintrude had requested earlier. She handed them to Cousin Lyris. Cousin Lyris gave one to Ermintrude, the other she kept. Rain looked at the table, where two plastic containers held the rice and peas and chicken that Ermintrude had given her earlier.

'You're ready to eat now?' her sister asked.

'No. Not yet.'

The nurse, who had turned away to the wide front doors of the building, paused to look back. 'She living on air, yes,' she commented. 'She hardly eats anything.'

'Hm.' Cousin Lyris looked at her young cousin. You could see it in those high, protruding cheekbones, no flesh on the face, nothing on the body. The grey dress hung on her like a sack. Grey! Rain always asked for grey. It was useless giving her another colour. She would accept it with thanks, with the same blank expression with which she received all gifts, but it would remain unused. She would never wear any other colour, the nurses said.

Suddenly, Rain started coughing. Deep, racking coughs that sounded like they were pulling her chest apart, tearing up her insides. She was bent double, Ermintrude holding her now. A nurse came to the door, tall, stout, kindly. 'All right,' she said, 'All right, Rain. Take it easy.' Cousin Lyris was standing, watching. Another nurse appeared in the doorway. Cousin Lyris walked towards them, drew the younger nurse inside.

'How she doing these days?'

'Very ill, and weak. Sometimes she just sits there dreaming, and talking to herself. One of the doctors was saying the other day that it might be an idea to send her back to the mental home.'

'What! Why? She not mad! Don't send her back there at all! She shouldn't have gone there in the first place; is just that she not talking to anybody. She not mad! And is in there she pick up this germ that have her tearing out her insides there now!'

The young nurse shrugged. Cousin Lyris persisted. 'You know that is inside that cold place she get this TB that have her here there?'

The nurse straightened the white apron over her blue uniform, put a hand to her cap. 'Well, Miss, I don't know.'

Cousin Lyris sighed. 'Is not your fault, anyway. But treat

her nice, you hear. Is because she have a lot on her mind that she so silent. Life didn't treat her nice. And she don't give any trouble?'

'No. She's no trouble, really. She just keeps to herself, and don't talk to anybody. Bright sunshine, everybody else outside, she want to be inside alone. She doesn't even sit on the verandah there, non. Inside here, or in her room most times.'

'Yes. Yes.'

'We always make joke and say that perhaps it have something to do with her name.'

Cousin Lyris didn't laugh. Just lifted her shoulders and said, 'Well!' Perhaps it had something to do with her name! She always wondered what had motivated her cousin Cora to call the child Rain. Her mother said that Cora had been seeing so much trouble with Andrew at the time, that when she got pregnant with Rain she thought it must be a blessing in disguise. And Emma said she had a suspicion that Rain was conceived one rainy night. She had been born on a day of brilliant sunshine, mid-day, 23rd December, 1929; Emma and Lyris, standing near to her bedside, had been amazed to hear her whisper, 'I want to call her Rain.' 'Rain!' they had exclaimed together. 'Rain', she had repeated, and then started to cry. Andrew had left for the States already that time, the month before. And Cora herself left the following year, when Rain was a cheeky, bubbly one-year-old. Lyris had been ill then, and she and her mother hadn't been able to keep both Ermintrude and Rain. Emma left to work in Trinidad soon afterwards. Rain had stayed first with Orilie, then, when she was about four, with their cousins Zebede and Dinah and then, when Dinah died suddenly, with Orilie again. They all said that Orilie was dissatisfied because she thought America should be hers because she was keeping the child! But perhaps it wasn't easy for her, too! Who knows? And then the father!

The coughing had stopped when Cousin Lyris went back out to the verandah. Ermintrude was holding Rain still, trying to get her to lean her head back. Rain pulled away. She didn't want to be touched. She leaned her head down on the table, breathing deeply, raspingly. Cousin Lyris approached. Touched her. Rain stiffened, shrugged her body away. Cousin Lyris spoke. 'You feeling better now?'

Rain looked up briefly, put out a hand, covered Cousin Lyris' hand with her own, and was quiet when Cousin Lyris placed a hand on her hair. After a while, she whispered, 'Take me to my room; take me to my room, please, Cousin Lyris.' And Cousin Lyris held her, wanting to cry for this woman who was still lost in a childhood she couldn't forget.

Because Rain couldn't forget. Most nights, while many of the other patients were asleep, she haunted the courtyard. The nurses didn't stop her. There was no danger. They sat and watched her from the verandah as she covered the distance between the encircling walls in long, urgent strides. She looked down on the winking lights of Paz from the porthole, disappeared from their sight as she turned and circled the courtyard, came back into view, striding.

Usually, Rain thought of the day that her . . . And her thoughts would jerk to a stop. She never knew what to call him, really. At the time she called him her father.

And Rain would look around quickly. Had anyone been close enough to see that thought? Sometimes she giggled. Stood and looked at the nurses. They hadn't heard. Suddenly unsafe in the space around her, Rain would stride back towards the verandah. Sometimes the nurses would walk to the room beyond, knowing that this woman whose pain they shared without understanding it, wanted to be left alone.

One night, at the far end of the corridor a woman sat, head on her hands, looking intently down between her knees. She wore a dress of fading yellow. Rain sat on the bench, looking at the ear peeping from between the encircling thumb and forefinger of the woman's left hand. She leaned forward, right hand folded in her lap, the left hand holding it securely at the wrist, and stared with frowning intentness at the ear. She squinted, trying to see it properly. Rain began to get agitated.

She leaned forward a little more, releasing her wrist and resting the palms of her hands on her legs. Rain darted a quick backward glance towards the door through which the nurses had disappeared. She didn't want anyone around to hear her thoughts.

Then she saw him. Perched on the railing just outside, just ahead of her. The cat paused, a shadowy black outline, looking directly at her. How long had he been looking? Had he heard? Rain burst out laughing, threw back her head and laughed long and loudly. He would know then that she didn't care anyway, whatever he might have thought he heard. Rain threw her head back against the grey wall, the thick black plait encircling her head and cushioning it against the wall. Her body shook so much that the bench teetered a little. Rain choked on her laughter.

A nurse came to the door and stood there for a moment looking, the only contrast to her grey uniform the white tracing the edge of the window. The plump nurse shook her head slightly, and turned back towards the room. It was after the nurses watched her movements on this strange night and reported to the doctor that he said perhaps she should go back to the mental home for a while.

Slowly, Rain lowered her head, looked through laughter-slit eyes towards the railing. He was gone. Abruptly, Rain's laughter stopped. The nurse peeped through the door and drew her head back inside. Rain looked from one side to the other. Listened. Looked around. Stood up and tiptoed to the banister. Looked down at the ground. Leaned out and looked around the corner. Smiled triumphantly. He was gone. Rain chuckled. She had fooled him.

But then, *he* had fooled *her*. She had so looked forward to his coming. She had never known him really. Not really. Not really. He *had* been back twice on holiday. Once when he came back she must have been . . . how old? Rain frowned, leaned back against the grey.

'Daddy coming!' She told everyone. That night, Miss

Orilie had opened the letter and stretched her mouth long like monkey backside. Rain giggled. Her friend Tisane always said that. Long like monkey backside – 'But Rain, what do you aunt, girl? How she like to stretch she mouth long like monkey backside so?' 'Aunt? Who aunt you talkin bout? Is not me aunt, non!' 'Well whoever aunt she is, she is a aunt with a monkey backside face.' 'Girl, Tisane, what does do you? Is why Miss say somebody go decatché you tail one day.' 'Ah chuts! Miss Mulroon face look like decatché!' 'Girl, Tisane!'

'What wrong wid you? What so good bout the world that you siddown dey laughin like Christ comin? What wrong wid you?'

Rain looked at the mouth stretched taut, at Miss Orilie's thin, long hands resting on the blue and white patterned plastic tablecloth, and wanted to laugh again. When the giggles came like that was the times that the Devil was around. 'You got the Devil with you?' Whenever she started giggling, they all asked her that. Miss Orilie, Auntie Myra, Uncle Anthony and even Cousin Mildred who managed to be warm and loving even though she had eight children of her own and three of other people's children living with her. 'You got the Devil with you?' So Rain set her face and stared past Miss Orilie's head straight into the Devil's eyes, daring him to make her laugh.

Look de Devil!
De Devil down dey!

In her thoughts, she sang straight into his face and dared him to come forward. Miss Orilie looked nervously over her shoulder, through the open doorway towards the trees outside. She looked back suspiciously at Rain. Sometimes she felt she really didn't like this child who stared and talked to herself and always seemed to have someone with her. She opened her mouth to ask, 'What wrong wid you?' But Rain saw the question coming and knew that it was always followed by the dreaded, 'You got the Devil wid you?' She must stop it. She could feel it in her bones that that would be unlucky as usual.

Pick up you bat, pick up you bat. Don't let her bowl that ball.

'You get letter from America today, Miss Orilie. Is me mother?'

'Don't be impertinent, child. Speak when you spoken to. Eh, so you smellin yourself, then? You is woman these days? You bigger than me in me own house?'

Rain bowed her head. Under the bench, she rubbed the big toe of her right foot against the hollow towards the back of her left foot.

She dipped her hand into the bowl of water, sprinkled the shirt and looked up just in time to see her spirit slip out of the room to stand shouting under the tree outside; this was its favourite spot for singing.

> *Boykin oh*
> *Boykin ay*
> *Searching for me boyking*
> *Boykin that cause the girl*
> *To go to the cemetery*
> *Boykin oh*
> *Boykin ay*
> *Searching for me Boyking*

'You hear what I say?'

'No, Miss Orilie.'

'How you mean, no Miss Orilie? You stand up right inside me nosehole an you don' hear what I say? I tell you already you will end up in trouble one day, you know. You never know what going on around you.'

Rain crossed her fingers against this curse. Never, she said to herself once. Never, she said again, looking into Miss Orilie's eyes. Never, she said to herself again, still staring at Miss Orilie, pleased that she had got through the third 'never' without interruption.

Miss Orilie fidgeted and sucked her teeth. If I say this child doesn' annoy me, I lie. I don't know where they find her, but she sure as hell got the Devil wid her.

'Is about you father. He say he comin on holiday.'

Lots of things rushed together. The envelope with its red, white and blue border. The red, white, and blue dress she had pulled from the suitcase below the bed on the day that Miss Orilie went to market. The red, white and blue dress with the slight stain on the hem because someone in the trace must have dropped something on it as the brown girl swung around the ring tra–la–la–la–la.

'Me father, Miss Orilie? He comin in truth?'

'If he comin in truth? So I dey in little children foolishness, then? I tell you you father comin you askin me if he comin in truth?'

Rain's big black eyes moved from the letter to Miss Orilie's face and back again.

'What he say, Miss Orilie?'

'Who "he"?'

'Me father.'

'Is you mother that write. Since when you know you father writin letter? Man doesn't write letter. Everything he have to say to you, you mother say it already.'

Rain thought of the boys who sat in school with her, pretending to write. She looked suspiciously at Miss Orilie. Tisane said that Miss Orilie look like she does make up some good lie sometimes. When she last saw her sister, Ermintrude had spoken of a letter from Daddy. A letter. And a doll brought over by someone on a visit from that magic place called Brooklyn. Two weeks later, a small parcel with a tiny white doll had arrived for Rain. Rain opened the parcel and shouted with joy, challenging Miss Orilie's tight, shuttered face with a laugh that made the lazy green lizard on the window forget the coveted fly and pause to stare in her direction.

'She pretty eh, Miss Orilie! She pretty, eh!'

Miss Orilie lifted her head from the letter. 'You mother send five dollars, too. And she say you must behave yourself.'

That time, too, Rain had asked, 'Me mother? Is me mother that write, Miss Orilie?'

'How you mean if is you mother that write? Look the letter there. It don't have nothing in it you eyes shouldn't see. Read it if you want.'

The nurses inside could hear Rain groaning, grinding her teeth. One of them walked out to the verandah and stood looking at her. 'Rain?' she said quietly. 'Rain?' But Rain was too far away to hear her. The nurse shook her head and walked away.

Her father had visited, but it seemed that he hardly came to Retreat to see them. He stayed most of the time in Victoria, where Ermintrude lived with Aunt Myra and Cousin Lyris. Rain would have liked to stay there, but Aunt Myra wasn't strong, and Cousin Lyris often ill. They couldn't have both children. Father – his name was Andrew, but at that time she always thought of him as Father, or my father – visited one Monday afternoon when she was outside washing the week's clothes. She didn't often go to school on a Monday, because Miss Orilie wanted her to do the washing then. But she had almost not done the washing that day, because the rain kept playing hide and seek with the sun. From morning, one minute it was drizzling, next minute, the sun was shining bright as ever.

> Rain coming, sun shining,
> The Devil and he wife fighting!

The Devil and his wife must have been having a hell of a fight that day. Rain wasn't sure which one was the Devil, the sun or the rain, and which was the wife, but up to now no-one was winning, because it was still drizzle, drizzle, then sun, sun.

Rain looked up when the man came into the yard. She didn't know who he was. The front door was closed, so he walked to the back of the house. She looked up from the washing, soap suds on her hands, wondering if the clothes would be dry in time so that she could iron tonight and so not

miss school tomorrow morning. If only the rain would just
go away and let the sun shine properly!

'Good afternoon.'

'Good afternoon, sir.'

'Is Miss Orilie in?'

'No, sir. She gone to Paz city today.'

'Do you know what time she will be back?'

'Well, she went this morning early, so she should be back
any time soon now.'

She stood there looking at the man, at his cream-coloured
shirt and grey pants. His black shoes were shining. He looked
like somebody who come from away. He looked nice, too.

'You want to leave a message for her, sir?'

'No. I'll wait a little.'

Rain didn't know what to do. Should she ask him to sit
inside? She didn't think Miss Orilie would like that. Tisane,
who told her everything that she heard from her own mother,
had said that she should be careful of strange men. And this
was a strange one. She had never seen him around. Well let
him stand up there. He walked to the front of the house.
From where she stood, she could see him leaning against the
mango tree. She pushed the bucket of water forward a little so
that she could see him better. He stood there looking down
the gap towards the road, the rough, unpainted board of the
kitchen looking even more rough against the smoothness of
his cream and grey neatness. He turned and saw her watching
him. Looked at her for a moment. Walked back to stand
looking at her.

'What is your name?'

'Rain.'

The man turned and walked back towards the mango tree.
He put a hand in his pocket, turned and walked back to her.

'You know Ermintrude?'

'Ermintrude? My sister Ermintrude?'

'Yes. I am her father.'

'Daddy! Daddy!' Soap suds and everything, she was fling-
ing her arms around him.

'All right, all right! You wettin me all over, man!'

'Daddy! Daddy!' She released him. 'But Daddy, why you didn't tell me? And I leave you standing up outside there. Come inside! Come inside, Daddy! When you come? Where is Ermintrude? She didn't come up with you? I longing to see her. How is Mammie? Why she didn't come with you? I really wish she did come with you. When you going back? Me and Ermintrude could come up and stay in Brooklyn with youall? You not going back to Victoria tonight? Bring me back there too if you going, eh, Daddy? I didn't know you reach, you know. But Miss Orilie did tell me you was coming!'

Rain was dancing, skipping, laughing, turning back to look at the sober-faced man who was following her inside. And who was actually her FATHER! He so handsome! Father in you shirt! Wait till I tell Tisane!

'Miss Orilie?' he said. 'Is your aunt, you know. You calling her Miss Orilie?'

'I don't like her, Daddy. She not nice. She don't like me. She tell me she don't like me. She tell me I growin tall, tall and trampin bout the place like a elephant. She tell me a lot of nasty things. I don't like her at all, Daddy. Bring me back to Brooklyn with you.'

Her father ran his hand along the plastic tablecloth.

'Miss Orilie tell your mother that you very rude. She say that you run away, that you use a lot of bad words and that you very difficult to control.'

Rain stared at him. Was he going to take Miss Orilie's side? Tisane had said that you couldn't depend on fathers; that usually they weren't there and visited only to shout and beat sometimes; Tisane had warned that on the whole children were better off without them. Rain found nothing sympathetic in his eyes; she looked down at the tablecloth.

'You staying tonight?'

'No. I going back to Victoria tonight. I will wait a while longer for Orilie.' He cleared his throat. 'You mother send you some things.' He picked up the brown bag and opened it.

'Some clothes and toys and books and things.'

You mother. He didn't show her anything that he had brought specially for her. When Miss Orilie came, they talked a lot; Rain stood in the doorway rubbing her big toe against the back of her left foot while her father told Miss Orilie stories about people in New York.

'Eh! You know I see allyou cousin Gaiphus there in New York?'

'Gaiphus? Eh! That alive!'

'Alive and kicking! And mamaguy!'

Rain had never heard Miss Orilie laugh like that before. Laugh and slap the table and choke laughing.

'Well meself I did good for he! Long before I meet him I hear people say that whenever you meet him, he trying to get a few cents off you!'

'Well, since here so he is, you know. And Cousin Melda, he mother, up the hill in the back over there, she like that too, you know! So he ain't take it far. Is like they say, cow doesn't make donkey.'

Rain couldn't help it. And how you mother manage? The thought leapt to her head with such force that she looked quickly at Miss Orilie's face. But she hadn't heard, of course. Is strange the way you could just think things about people and they go on sitting down there listening like nothing happen.

'Well Mr Gaiphus meet the right one! Those fellas say when you see you bounce him up, if he didn't marry last week, he getting married next week, and he asking for a contribution.'

'Oh yes? Gaiphus bright! He ain't fraid somebody sue him for breach of contract in this New York dey!'

'Well he ain't giving nobody the chance because he ain't naming no name! An you know meet I meet Gaiphus, he tell me he getting married, in truth.'

'Woy-o-yoy!'

'Well I couldn't believe it, you know. I say them fellas did jokin, but Gaiphus tell me he getting married, and he ask for,'

Rain's father dropped his voice, 'a little thing, you know. A small forty dollars or so, just to help out.'

Miss Orilie leaned back in her chair, choking with laughter.

'Well you don't know I coulda take Gaiphus and fling him quite in Ohioho! Anyway, I tell him I want to meet the bride. I stand up there and carry on asking him a whole heap of questions about what she look like, and say that on behalf of the family, you know, I want to meet her. He leave so fast, eh!'

Miss Orilie actually giggled.

'He must be still in some street in New York trying to get some lady to come and meet me! Me ain't know! That is the last I hear bout the nastiness!'

'Yes! Well that is a good one!' Miss Orilie turned her head to the side to wipe the tears from her eyes, and caught sight of Rain slouching in the doorway. 'Don't stand up there listening to big people conversation, child. Go and find something to do!'

Rain looked at her father. But he said not a word. Just sat there chuckling as he remembered the man in New York. So Rain lowered her head and turned away. She sat on the step and listened to their talk and laughter. Nothing to do with her. He stayed two weeks, but that was the only time he visited her, and it was as if he hadn't really visited her. Fathers were like that, Tisane said. But she heard him talking to Miss Orilie about Ermintrude, about how well Ermintrude was doing in school, about how Ermintrude had grown, about how they were trying to get Ermintrude to go up to the States. He said that Ermintrude was just like him.

'That girl, eh! If you see her play netball, man. Is true she don't have much height but when you see she hold on to that ball on the court, nothing can't get past her, non. The best thing on the court, yes!'

'Mmmm.'

'She remind me of me in my days, man. I was looking smaller than some of them fellas; some of them big and all six foot and more, but when you see I ketch on to that ball, man, ten o them so to catch me. Swift, swift on the field, man! And style!'

'Yes,' said Miss Orilie admiringly. 'I always hear you was a good footballer. People does still talk you name!'

'Man what do you man! I wasn't joking, you know!'

Rain peeped through the door behind Miss Orilie's back and looked at her father. He was looking up at the ceiling and stroking his chin. She almost thought, Eh! He just think he nice! but held it back just in time. After a while she stopped hearing what they were saying. She put her head down on her knees and tried to imagine what America looked like. She thought about her mother. She waited for her father to say, 'Rain! Come here, girl! Come and talk to you father!' Then all of a sudden she heard him saying, 'I must really go now, yes. It getting late.' She lifted her head and listened. He didn't even call her! Rain dashed away from the steps and under the house. Miss Orilie called and she didn't answer. And he just said, 'All right then, tell her I gone.' That was all. Tell her I gone.

She ran away that night. Ran all the way down to Tisane's house in the trace. Stumping her foot against the roots of the trees in the darkness. But she didn't even feel it. She lay down on the bed with Tisane and her brothers and sisters and cousins and listened to them talking and laughing and telling stories for a long, long time. They made jokes about everything, about Old Man Mody who shouted from his verandah when they teased his dog, Mody who stood on his verandah every morning and afternoon to keep watch over his julie and tin mango trees as the school children went by. Some of them defied him, jumped across the drain, seized a fallen mango and ran away laughing while he shouted and the dog barked. They watched the rotting mangoes and wondered why he threatened to poison them rather than allow children to eat them. They decided that he hated children, and invented gruesome stories about his dealings with the Devil to explain this hatred. Rain knew that if she hadn't been so sad, they would have compared him to Orilie, knowing that she wouldn't mind. But they didn't want to make her feel worse. And knowing this only made her want to cry more. But it also made her want to stay with them. So she listened and smiled when they talked about Eileen who always talked to herself, and who threatened to send their 'backsides to thy Kingdom come' when they passed and hit at the fence in front of her house with thick sticks.

In the midst of the laughter, Tisane's mother called out, 'Rain, time for you to go home now. Miss Orilie must be wondering where you is.' And Rain shouted back without enthusiasm, 'Yes, Cousin Mildred, I going now.'

Then Tisane looked at her friend's face, put a finger to her lips and drew Rain out of the room. The others heard Rain's voice call out, 'Good night, Cousin Mildred.'

'All right, child, say good night for me, eh!'

'Yes, Cousin Mildred. All right, Tisane girl.'

'All right then, Rain, see you tomorrow, eh!'

Two minutes later, both girls tiptoed into the room. Tisane placed an urgent finger on her lips and motioned to her relatives to continue talking.

Rain was gone early the following morning, before Cousin Mildred was awake. She walked up the hill and into the yard, bold as brass. Miss Orilie decided, 'Well today, today self I killing this child. Rain, where you come from?'

Miss Orilie stripped her naked to beat her with the peas whip, so that there would be no clothes in the way. Rain took the beating without flinching, making no sound. Frustrated, Miss Orilie screamed at her. 'Little woman like you bringing child in people door mouth before they know what happening. Eight years you have, and you stayin out already. Oh Lord, I have no children of me own to give me this kind of crosses. Why people don't sit down and mind their children after they make them? Is me they put sit down here to have all this problems with you! Oh Lord me God, well I kill priest? Jesus, deliver me from this burden! I don't want no little whore in me yard, you hearin me?'

'I could put on me clothes now, Miss Orilie?'

'Child if I say I don't hate you, I lie. Nothing, nothing good could ever come out of you. You curse. Beg God pardon, child, but you well curse.'

And Rain had looked at Miss Orilie with dead eyes and thought of Ben down the road, Ben who walked and dribbled on himself and couldn't even talk properly, and who people said had been cursed by his aunt because he had stolen her clean-neck fowl. And Rain stared at Miss Orilie hard and thought, The curse will fall right back on you, because God self see I didn't do nothing, and I didn't thief nobody clean-neck fowl! You cursing yourself, Orilie. And even as she thought it, she called on Papa God to witness it, and to witness that she hadn't done anything, so no curse shouldn't take her.

And later there was Sister. Miss Orilie's only child was born when Rain was nine. Tisane said, 'Rain, girl, everybody wondering where this child come out. Nobody didn't know Miss Orilie in this kind of thing still. I hear Mammie say that Orilie almost hitting fifty.'

'Tisane, girl, they going jail you, you know.'

'Is me mouth they going jail. They won't catch me at all.'

After Sister was born, Rain hardly went to school. She had to take care of Sister and of the house while Miss Orilie worked. When Miss Orilie was at home now, she showered her love on Sister, kissing her, hugging her, playing with her. At first, Rain would pinch Sister and make her scream when they were alone together. Then when Sister was old enough to tell her mother, Rain stopped, and kept the cold hatred inside of her, talking about it only to Tisane.

'Girl Tisane, Orilie think she child is the best thing since fry bakes!'

'You don't find she look like a fry bakes in truth? Watch round she mouth how it does be white! You know when you put the bakes in the hot oil but the oil not plenty, so round the edge stay white, white?'

Rain giggled. Trust Tisane! And Tisane said, 'Don't study Orilie, girl! That is not people to study!'

Rain wrote often to her mother, and still to her father sometimes. Her mother wrote all the time, sent her clothes that Rain never wore, because there was no place to wear them to. She spoke of money which she sent to Miss Orilie, so that Rain could be properly taken care of. She told Rain she loved her; she told Rain to be good; sometimes Rain sat staring at the letters and wondering what love looked like; sometimes she took the letters to Tisane; Tisane read them and said, 'You mother love you, girl. She just out there trying to make a better life for you.'

'That is what she say, Tisane. But how she out there could make a better life for me?'

'She going send for you when she could afford. She say that too.'

When Rain was fourteen, she talked to Miss Orilie about going out to look for a job. She wanted to sew, she said. At school, they used to tell her it was her best subject, and Miss Orilie knew that she could sew things well.

'Job? What job? You inside here good, good, helping me out, now you talking about job? Is hot you little tail hot so, is man you want to go and look for! What job?'

Rain opened her eyes to a face bending over her. 'Move, Orilie,' she shouted. 'Get outa me way!'

The nurse stepped back. Rain focused. 'Nurse,' she said uncertainly, 'Nurse?' Then she smiled weakly. 'Sorry, Nurse. I thought was a diablesse.'

Nurse Jones was thinking of this now as she watched Rain's cousin lead her towards the room. Was Rain really losing her mind now, she wondered? She walked quickly ahead of them and straightened the sheet.

'Thanks, Nurse,' said Cousin Lyris.

'I will lie down for a while, Cousin Lyris. I just feeling a little bit weak, but I'll be okay soon.'

'Don't worry about it. Rest yourself. We will stay for a while, because we not getting the bus until later.'

'Stay in here then, for a while, non. I might sleep, but you could stay with me, if you want.'

Rain closed her eyes immediately. Cousin Lyris sat on a chair near to the bed, whispering to the nurse that she should tell the others to go ahead and eat. The nurse smiled and left the room. People always say these nurses unhelpful, thought Cousin Lyris, but I must say these here really kind to Rain. And you could see she like them, too. Cousin Lyris sighed. Rain lived everything so intensely, had so longed for her parents, that Lyris knew that her waking moments were caught up in painful memories. Perhaps she didn't even escape them when she slept.

Ermintrude visited her one day; Rain was always pleased to see her sister, but she never showed it now. Ermintrude was always happy, always bubbling with some story, and Rain's sad eyes made her uncomfortable. Rain always stood straight and tall, staring down into your eyes when you told her something, and she never seemed to see the joke in things.

'Rain,' said Ermintrude, 'our father is coming next month.'

'Our mother said she might be coming. She coming too?'

'No. Daddy said she can't make it. She can't get enough time off from work.'

'Daddy write you?'

'Yes.'

'He does write you often?'

'Sometimes.'

'He never write me, you know Ermine. Before, it was because you were older and I was very young. But I bigger now. He must know I bigger now.'

Ermintrude lifted her shoulders.

'Ah well! I suppose I wasn't even born yet when he leave; so is you he know, really, and not me. You was big already, ent?'

'Yes. I was almost six when he left. Rain, when he visit this time, he will . . . he might . . . I mean, he intend for me, for us, I think, to go back with him.'

'To Brooklyn?' Rain's eyes were suddenly alight. 'Ermine,

you don't mean he want us to go to Brooklyn? Ermine, you jokin!'

Ermine looked miserable. 'Is true, yes, Rain.'

'But, Ermine, girl, you joking! And you saying that easy so? You ent glad?'

'Yes. Of course I glad.'

'Auntie Myra don't want you to go?'

'Yes, yes. Auntie Myra glad. She and Cousin Lyris say they will miss me, but they feel it have better opportunities for me out there. I will miss them, too, but I really want to see me mother again.'

'Girl, Ermine, I not going miss nobody. Exceptin Tisane. That ole Orilie is a nasty, mean, good-for-nothing, backside-hole . . .'

'Rain!'

'Let we don't talk bout she, girl!' Rain flung her arms wide. 'Woy! We going America.' Then she looked at Ermintrude's miserable face. 'What happen, Ermine? What happen?'

Ermintrude shook her head. 'Nothing.'

'Is both of us that going, Ermine? Or is you alone?'

'No. Is both of us, Rain.'

Rain told Tisane. 'Me father coming, girl. And guess what, non, Tisane!'

'What?'

'Guess, non.'

'He promise to kill Orilie.'

Rain sucked her teeth, laughing.

'Well I don't know what else could make you look so!' Tisane, now in her second year at high school, looked at her friend and hoped it was something special.

'Me and Ermintrude going back with him!'

'You joking!'

Rain danced, circling the tree under which Tisane was sitting in the yard. Tisane shouted. Then, watching her friend, she suddenly remembered the last time Rain's father had visited. 'But anyway, girl, remember to happy for yourself, eh!'

'How you mean?'

Tisane picked up a twig from the ground and broke it. She couldn't explain her fear; couldn't explain that her friend's eyes sometimes frightened her; she didn't know how to say that she was afraid, sometimes, because of the way Rain loved her parents and felt so sure being with them meant happiness. It wasn't that, really, it was just the way that Rain loved and hated so deeply, and let it into her eyes. Tisane's mother always said, 'Don't wait on nobody to make you happy; especially not no man. Man, them is the most mix-up set of people the good Lord ever create! Dem does only think bout theyself.' And sometimes when she was vexed about something and quarrelling to herself she would say, 'Dem blasted man always thinkin dem is God gift to woman. Never could see further than they blasted nose. The moment you let them know how much you like them you in trouble! Is to keep out of their way and happy for youself! Take you happiness outa de general world and don't wait on no one person to make you happy. Dem!'

'I mean, well, don't wait on nobody else to make you happy; just decide for yourself what you going to do get happy for yourself.' Tisane hesitated. 'You know what I mean?'

'Girl, is me sewing I like already. I going just do that when I go to Brooklyn. And Ermintrude say it will have opportunities to learn more about it there. And Ermintrude like sewing too, you know. So perhaps we might be able to work together or something. O gosh, Tisane, girl, I can't wait!'

'Girl, I happy for you, girl.'

Lyris' thoughts were on that fateful visit Rain's father had made to Paz. Sometimes, she thought, watching Rain's twitching face, and pushing up her glasses, I believe if we could see the future, we would do plenty things different. But then that is a wasted thought! A wasted thought!

Andrew Darling sailed into Paz City on the boat on a day that was unusually cool for the city – sixty-nine degrees. It was December, one week before Christmas, and shoppers were busy as he drove with his brother through the crowded streets. They drove straight to Victoria, where his brother lived. He stayed a day or two with Anthony, the only member of his family still alive on the island. Then he went to Aunt Myra, which was where he really considered home when he was in Paz.

'You getting prosperous, boy!' Aunt Myra greeted him. 'The stomach pushing out.'

'Is problems yes, Aunt Myra. Is problems that have it looking so.'

'Come, come, let me pinch you for good luck, so I could get some of this problem. Yes, boy. You looking well good.'

'You must introduce me to this problem and them, boy! You think is today I lookin for some problems so?'

'Lyris! You find them already, girl! How you looking nice so? She getting younger, Aunt Myra? Something, or somebody treatin her well. Watch her, non!'

'I treatin myself well! I not waiting on nobody to decide if they go treat me well! Is why I lookin good so!'

'So where me daughter? Where allyou hidin her?'

'Hm! If we want to hide daughter, we waiting until you pass by here, then? She doing a job for the Sampsons, so she over there. She should be back soon, though. It almost four already. She usually here by half-past.'

'What job is that?'

'You daughter is a big-time seamstress, yes.'

'Mmm-hmm?' Andrew's eyes were bright with pleasure.

'All kinds of orders coming here for her. She have all the Sampsons' sewing for the holidays, so she there finishing up curtains, I think, today.' Lyris pushed the glasses higher on her nose, placed her arms akimbo again. 'Then last week she was doing the same thing for those fair-skin people up the hill there, the, er, how you call them again? You know who I mean, Mammie. Those that come from England last year.'

'Oh, the Hosein people.'

'That's right. You remember you went to school with

some fair-skinned children who used to live along the trace by
the stand-pipe?'

'Er . . .' Andrew considered.

'Well, the younger ones, the boys, would have been your
age-group. I went to school with the two girls.' Lyris sucked
her teeth and frowned trying to recall something. 'They had a
name they used to call them . . . Babadee!' she shouted,
remembering.

'Oh, Babadee! Little Babadee! and Big Babadee! They here?
Ay! Me daughter sewing for these Babadee people an them? I
know Babadee, yes. Little Babadee used to play football with
me! At least he used to *try*!' Andrew chuckled. 'He wasn't in
me class at all.' He stroked his thinning hair. 'Yes, man. I
know Babadee. Is *dem* Ermintrude working for?'

'Is not Babadee as you used to know them, non. I hear they
come into some good money, so they living in style!'

'Eh-heh? An you ain't find out where they get it?'

'You can't get yours so, boy. Apparently they had family
in Trinidad that die out, and leave them well comfortable.'

'Well I wonder if I ain't have a family hide somewhere?'

Aunt Myra shook her head. 'Your race of people never
have plenty children. Look you only brother there. Not one.
So is only yours to continue the line.'

Andrew stretched, settling back into the armchair. 'Well I
really glad to hear me daughter doing so well. She will go far
with that over there, too. She don't have to go in nobody
house and beg them for their job. I hear Cora saying that she
must make inquiries about a place for her, because of what
you tell her about the sewing, you know. But I don't think
she realise that is high, high level we girl dealing with, you
know.'

'So how Cora now, Andrew?'

'Well girl, is one day good, one day bad. She have to go
into the hospital all the time for them to put her on this
machine, you know. And sometimes she don't leave the bed
for weeks. And this new complaint we tell you about just
complicate matters. But these last days she been working

little bit.' Andrew sighed. 'But to tell you the truth, I don't believe she have long to go again.'

Myra made the sign of the cross. 'God help her! My best niece, yes! A good, good child! Well, we in the Lord hands! Because when people take with this complaint, is the end really! God knows best!'

Lyris made the sign of the cross, and kissed her hand. 'Lord spare her! Well, if is so it is!' She smoothed the tablecloth. 'If it is so it is already!' She lifted her shoulders and tried to change the subject. 'You hungry?'

'No. I eat by Anthony not long ago.'

'You must tell those children, you know, Andrew. We never tell Ermintrude about the mother illness, and I sure Rain don't know anything.'

'Yes. I will tell her. And,' Andrew cleared his throat, moved restively in the chair, uncrossed his legs one way and crossed them back the other way, 'I have to talk to Rain, too.'

'Yes, you must tell her about the mother. They should know, especially now they going up, too.'

'Well, to tell you the truth,' Andrew uncrossed his legs, cleared his throat, 'I been wondering if I don't better leave Rain still and only take Ermintrude.'

'You can't do that!' Lyris came to sit in the chair opposite him. She pushed up her glasses, fixing her myopic eyes on his face.

'No!' said Aunt Myra at the same time, sitting on the dining-room chair to his left, her head turned so that she could fix her eyes on his face. One plait was outside of the confines of the headtie, pointing forward over her round face like an exclamation point. 'You can't do that, my son.'

'She know she going already, you know. That will kill her. And we buy the tickets and get their passport and everything with the money youall send. What is the problem now?'

Andrew was silent. He sat with his head down, then put his head back and remained looking at the ceiling. They waited for him to speak. Myra watched the dog slinking through the sitting-room with its head down. What new trouble is this

now? she wondered. They say you doesn't give us more than
we can handle, yes, Papa God, but what new trouble is this
now?

Myra turned her head to look again at Andrew. Watched
the way he was staring at his hands.

'You can't do that, son,' said Myra. 'That child living in
hell at Orilie. Is me niece, but she not the kind of people you
suppose to leave your children by. She not a *people* person.
Everybody have their calling, and Orilie is just not a people
person, that's all.'

Andrew sighed, put his head back again and looked up at
the ceiling, biting his bottom lip. The women watched him.

'You know some people just don't make for that?' Aunt
Myra continued. 'Well that is Orilie. In fact now that Emma
home, I hear is more so by there Rain does be, and Orilie vex,
vex as a result. So is more unpleasantness. You can't leave her
there at all.' Aunt Myra pulled the ends of her headtie,
tightening it. 'God going punish you! That child grow up by
Orilie barely knowing how to read, and she bright, you
know. You can't leave her there.' Aunt Myra turned around
on the chair. Turned back to look at Andrew. 'And she think
the world of you, you know. This one here always talking
bout you, too. And on the few occasions you see that they
manage to get together, when I hear them talking, you name
always in the conversation, yes. Is a *Daddy this* and a *Daddy
that*!' Aunt Myra sucked her teeth, stood up and walked to the
door. 'What you sayin at all, Andrew? What is dis at all?'

'All right, Mammie,' said Lyris, 'remember what the
doctor say; don't get too excited now.'

Andrew sighed, started cracking the fingers of his left hand
with the thumb of his right. He drew a deep breath and stood
up, walked to the door and put his arm around Aunt Myra's
shoulder.

'Aunt Myra, come and sit down. Sit down here.' He let her
sit in the armchair where he had been sitting. Pulled forward
the straight-backed chair and sat facing her. He looked to his
left where Lyris sat in the other chair. Shifted his chair around

slightly so that he had them both within his range of vision. 'Lyris, youall wouldn't like this! But I feel I have to say it!' And before they could pull their thoughts together, he added, 'Rain is not my child.'

Aunt Myra and Lyris stared at him. '*Maliwése!*' Aunt Myra exclaimed, leaing forward closer to his face.

Lyris spoke. 'What you saying at all? What you saying at all, Andrew?'

Andrew kept his head bowed, looking at the brown floor-boards beneath his feet. He felt miserable. He had carried a bitterness inside him for all these years, had quarrelled with Cora about it at first, and then, when she became ill eight years ago, he had stopped. But the bitterness was always inside him. Even before she joined him in the States all those years ago, he had written her an angry letter about it, and she had returned an equally angry one of denial.

'Where you going with this lie?' asked Aunt Myra quietly. 'Cora tell you that Rain is somebody else child?'

'Aunt Myra, the time when . . .'

'I ask you something. Cora tell you that?'

'No, Aunt Myra.'

'Well where you going with this lie?'

'Aunt Myra, you must have known the problems me and Cora were having around that time.'

'Yes, I know you used to beat her,' Aunt Myra said, gripping the arms of her chair. 'I know that she run away more than once to hide from you because those times you had so much hatred in you heart.'

'It wasn't hatred, Aunt Myra, is just problems.'

'The problems was both of allyou own. Both of allyou couldn't find food to put in those children mouth. Is marasma that kill the first little one. I know that. But woman doesn't beat man and go on like beast when trouble take them.'

'But me is man. Is me that suppose to provide.'

'Look you have a daughter now who providing for sheself with she sewing. And when man nor woman can't provide, the problem is both of them own. I don't know where youall get this habit raising allyou hand on woman. It have all to do with wickedness and nothing to do with providing. But that is not the point. The point is that she run away from you enough times to save sheself, but I put me head on a block to say that she never lie down in nobody else bed.'

'Auntie Myra . . .'

'And you can't tell me nothing to make me believe that happen!'

'But what it is make you say that, Andrew?'

'Lyris, that was a time that Cora go for three weeks, I don't know where she is. Then soon after she come back, she pregnant. That child not mine, Lyris. I know.'

'*Maliwése!*'

'Don't curse me, Aunty Myra! You don't know how I suffer with this thing inside me!'

'*You* don't know how *she* suffer!' Aunt Myra sat back, turned right and made a spitting sound. '*Maliwése!*' She placed her hands on the arms of the chair and pushed herself to her feet.

'But Andrew, what Cora say?'

'Is a long time I didn't talk to her about it, but from the beginning I tell her is not my child.'

'Yes, and you nearly kill her when you tell her that where she lie down pregnant there!'

'So you know.'

'Yes, and I know that you beat her again until you nearly beat the child out of her stomach. I never understand why she didn't leave you then, and then I thought you change. And now I realise that you can't teach old dog new tricks! *Pa maliwése*, Andrew Darling!'

'Auntie Lyris! I mean, Auntie Myra!'

'I not you aunt, don't call me auntie!'

'Mammie! Mammie, take it easy!'

'Auntie Myra, since after those days, I never lay a finger on Cora to beat her. We live good, but she know I never accept Rain as my child, I accept that is my fault, that I drive her to it, but I never accept Rain as my child. Since after she sick, I never talk to her about it again, and she don't know that I will tell Rain now, but . . .'

'That you will what? Andrew Darling, leave my doormouth this minute! Right this minute! Get out, I say!'

'Mammie! Mammie, no! We have to talk about it!'

'Get out!' Auntie Myra was staring at Andrew, her eyes big and round, pointing towards the door.

'Mammie!' Lyris went to her, put her arms around her shoulders, drew her away from the door. Andrew stood up. 'Don't go, Andrew, wait!'

'What!' Myra pulled away. 'So you defying me in my own house, then? Giving the reprobate right to stay?'

Andrew stood with bowed head. Lyris led her mother away. Motioned to Andrew to wait. In the room, she sat with her mother on the bed. 'Mammie! Mammie, listen. We can't make him go.'

'*You* can't make him go. Me? I . . .'

'Mammie, think about Rain.'

'Oh God!' Myra's shoulders shook. She put her face in her hands and sobbed.

'Mammie, this will kill Rain. If he leave her here and then tell her that to boot, think of what going happen to her!'

'We will have to take her. We manage all these years with Ermintrude, we could make it with Rain. We will have to take her.'

'Mammie, we still have to try to make him see he shouldn't tell her that, and that he should take her back with them. Don't make him go, Mammie. Think about Rain.'

So Andrew stayed. He looked ashamed, but it was as if he had to talk about the cancer that had been eating him all of these years. As if he felt he couldn't sit down there and let everybody think he stupid. Later, they sat in the kitchen outside while he talked to Ermintrude. He was so proud of her. Kissed her and told her how proud he was that she was doing so well. Myra couldn't look at all of this, knowing that Rain would have none of it.

'But, Mammie, Rain look so much like his family. The

height, the face, everything.'

'Child, you don't hear the worst of it. The person who Andrew believe is Rain father is his brother Anthony. I suppose Andrew feel that with her height and everything, is more Anthony she look like.'

'What!'

'Now remember that Anthony and Andrew is same father, not same mother. All of them grow up in this area here. I never tell you the half of it, but was around the time you was in Carriacou staying that the whole thing develop. When Cora growing up, young lady in me dead sister Alma house, God rest her soul, Anthony start coming round. But Cora never like him, so nothing never go ahead, you know what I mean.'

'Yes?'

'When Andrew appear on the scene, now, like a shot out of a gun, before you know it, she and Andrew pick up and they getting married.'

'So there was never anything between she and Anthony?'

'Not to my knowing. Cora never had time for him. But people say heself never had eyes for nobody else. Now time pass, hard times come and hit us, Andrew who was so nice before get like beast, and he really used to beat that little girl. Was a shame. That time when Andrew talking about, dey, when she leave his house, is here she did come, because by this time now Alma dead and is me she was closest to. But run she run come here, meself say, well you know is here first he go look for you, this is not place to hide.' Myra sighed, took off her headtie, replaced it. 'Oh God, eh! Oh Jesus! What trouble is dis now?'

'All right, Mammie. All right. Take it easy.'

'So we talk bout it, and the two of us decide that is for her to go some place he wouldn't expect. That time Anthony was moving with Eliza in the trace. I walk over there with her meself; we pass in the back up the hill. Eliza say all right, she could stay there. So is by Eliza she come and end up, stay there three weeks. But I don't know what say, who tell him what. Sometimes I wonder if is Eliza sheself that say thing, you know, knowing how Anthony did always feel about Cora. But when Cora tell me what Andrew think, I say but how is that he reach thinkin dey? You tell him something? Anything happen with you and Anthony?'

Lyris pushed up her glasses, eyes on her mother's face, mouth half-opened.

'And she say to me, never! Not before Andrew, not after! And she put she neck on a block that even self she had that in mind she wouldn't go in the woman house and take her man from her! And I believe her! I don't know who say what, who put thing in Andrew head, but Cora is the kind of person who never fraid nobody, and if she did ever make mistake do a thing like that, she wouldn't of fraid to take she medicine. Eight years ago, when she know she ill, and they saying she could dead anytime, she write me and say that Andrew still believe Rain not his, but if she dead tomorrow, she want me to know that she never lie down with nobody else, so if not his, is God own! And that is not thing people saying easy!'

'You ever tell him that?'

'Never. This time there is the first time we ever talk bout it, because heself never bring up the subject and I don't want to interfere, but Cora tell me in the letter all those years ago that she tell him; she tell him just what you hear she tell me there; but is what he have in he head already is that he want to believe.'

'But how? Why?'

'Child, man strange. And Andrew not no different. Is he pride. He grow up with a big name in this area because of the football. Was a bright young man. One time before Cora he used to go with Alpheus daughter dey, the one that in Trinidad now. She come and get pregnant. Andrew never did want the child, I understand, but he come and accept it, and then when people look at the child, everybody bawl blue murder. Because the little girl was the spitting image of Andrew best friend. Nobody didn't have to ask question. Was the stamp of the man. The whole village laugh, and everybody used to tease say how he get a six for a nine. I think Andrew never forget that, so anytime it have a shadow of a doubt, I suppose he want to be sure to save face. Is he pride, child. Is nothing but he stupid pride eating him.'

'But to that extent?'

'Man is the strangest nation. And Cora self have she ways too, you know. She very secretive. Just through not wanting to talk about things, she used to keep the stupidest things from Andrew, so he always feel things have more in it than is really there. And I think he only find out where she was afterwards because somebody else tell him. So he must come and feel the thing had more in it than it really had. And you know man. The moment them is friend with a woman is usually one thing they want. And Andrew know heself. So he must be come and feel is only one reason why his brother help out Cora. Child, Cora and Rain just paying for what he feel somebody else do him. That is my feeling.'

Lyris sighed. Rain's face was still twitching, and Lyris knew that hers was not a restful sleep. None of them was feeling restful during this visit. Sitting outside, looking at Sister who had come back to the verandah and was standing looking out towards the high walls which hid Paz from view, Ermintrude tried to keep back the tears. It hurt that her sister couldn't stand her touch. Her most painful memory was that conversation with her father long ago.

She couldn't believe what he was saying to her. 'Daddy, whatever you do, don't tell Rain that. She always look forward to hearing from you, Daddy. She always wonder why you don't write her, and I never know what to say. The last time, after you write and tell me that you mightn't take her up, I try to tell her, but in the end I even had to lie and tell her she definitely going too, Daddy. I couldn't tell her, Daddy. Whatever you do, don't tell her you not her father, Daddy. It going kill her.'

'Ermintrude, child, try and understand. It hurt me, too, but I have to. I can't pretend so.'

'What Mammie say?'

'You mother don't know. That is something else I didn't tell you, Ermintrude. You mother very ill. She has a kidney complaint. She been like that for a lot of years now. That is why she never take the chance to come out here on holiday. And lately it get complicated with other things. The doctors say she have, er, she have,' he looked at his daughter and lowered his voice almost to a whisper, 'cancer. She not expected to live for long.'

'Oh God!' Ermintrude started to cry. 'Oh God! Oh God, me mudder! Woy!' She was sobbing, wiping away the tears and sobbing again.

'All right, Ermine. I know how you feel, chile. All of us feel so. But I couldn't tell you before.'

'And Daddy, you going tell Rain all of that? You so wicked? You going tell Rain all of this?'

'Child!'

'No! No! Noooo! Daddy, you so wicked? Oh God, no!'

'Ermintrude! Don't pull away from me, Ermintrude. Listen, baby. Dry you eyes. All right! All right!' And he put his arms around her, rocking her quiet. 'All right, baby? Everything will be all right. I know it will make you happy, so Rain will go up with us, then. But she have to know the other things, Ermintrude. She have to know.'

Aunt Myra said afterwards that Rain died inside in that December of 1944. Andrew said that she took it well. After she heard his story, she just sat and stared at him. She stared at him and was almost straining to hear his voice because the rain was beating so hard against Miss Orilie's galvanize that day. December was always like that. Very cold, and lots of rain. It was the time when things were really bearing. Rain looked out of Miss Orilie's window at the trees growing at the side of the house. The green peas were ready now for eating. Miss Orilie would have a good crop this year. Rain had asked Andrew Darling one favour. Not to tell Miss Orilie. He assured her that he had spoken only to Ermintrude, Aunt Myra and her Cousin Lyris. He would tell no-one else.

Rain did not even go to say goodbye to Tisane. Tisane couldn't believe this. She knew that something was wrong. She didn't go to Miss Orilie, but wrote afterwards to Myra Augier, of Victoria, putting in brackets after the name, Ermintrude's aunt, just in case that wasn't really the surname. Myra answered the letter, saying that Rain had specially asked her to say goodbye to Tisane, that she was sure Rain would have wanted to say goodbye herself, but that something had made her very unhappy before she left.

Myra and Lyris would never forget Rain's eyes those last days of December, when she should have been happy about celebrating her fifteenth birthday. She had returned with her father, to stay for three days before their departure. She greeted Ermintrude as though she wasn't really seeing her; when she inclined her head and said, 'Good evening, Aunt Myra,' her eyes remote and looking just beyond her great aunt's ear, Myra burst into tears and pulled her into her arms.

'Come, child. Don't believe everything you hear, you see? Is not true, child. You mother tell me is not true, and I believe her. And anyway it don't matter, Rain. Who you is, is who you is. Always remember that. Rain, my child, it don't matter. Is not true, and we don't love you no less.'

'Is not true, Rain,' Lyris repeated, 'Whatever you father believe because he and you mother was in confusion, is not true.'

When Myra drew back and looked into her niece's face, it was as if the child hadn't heard. Her eyes were remote. 'Rain,' she said, shaking her slightly. 'Rain, child.'

'Is all right, Auntie Myra. Is all right, you know.' Rain's voice was soothing, as though she were consoling her great aunt about something else. Perhaps she is, thought Myra, who know? Perhaps she is. Myra stood at the door and looked over far away at the hills behind Clozier. The tops of those mountains seemed to have absorbed all the mist from the Grand Etang this morning. Lord, Myra said to herself, I wish sometime you would explain the trials and tribulations you bring to bear on us. But that must be too much to ask,

Lord! But this time I can't see how, non. I just can't see how. Forgive me, Lord, but like Thomas this time I have to say, 'Help my unbelief!'

Before they left the house, they heard Myra speak quietly to Andrew, 'Andrew Darling, tell me one thing. After Cora reach back to you house that time, you didn't have any dealings with her?'

'How you mean, Auntie Myra?'

'We is big people, Andrew Darling. You sleep with you wife in those days? You have sex with her? You make love to her?'

'Auntie Myra, Cora is me wife. I love her then and I love her now. We sleep together, yes. We make love.'

'And still you saying what you saying?'

Andrew looked uneasy. 'Auntie Myra, Cora stay away from me for three weeks! You know she never even tell me where she was? I take a lot. I take the blame because I did treating her bad. But nobody not making me look like a fool.'

'And that is all making you say what you saying? The fact that she stay away from you for three weeks?'

Andrew sighed. Auntie Myra felt that there was something he wasn't saying, that somebody had poisoned his mind. Whoever it is, she thought, going to have to answer to God. Watching them, Lyris crossed her fingers, knowing that her mother wanted to curse Andrew again. Myra opened her mouth to tell Andrew never to cross her doormouth again, but changed her mind and decided not to add to the hatred that touching so much things already. But she knew she wouldn't be able to forgive him for this.

Myra and Lyris went to see them off. The last thing Rain said to her aunt and cousin was, 'Auntie Myra, Cousin Lyris, if you ever see my friend Tisane, tell her I say goodbye for me.' She turned back to say, 'Tisane was really nice. Don't forget to tell her if you see her, eh.'

Myra and Lyris were crying too much to respond as the three walked up the gangway and into the ship. Ermintrude and Andrew turned and waved. Myra and Lyris did not return the wave. They were waiting for Rain, walking behind the two, straight-backed and tall, to turn and wave. Rain walked into the ship without a backward glance.

Two months later, there was news of Cora's death. Myra wrote to say that perhaps Rain should come home. She could stay with her and Lyris.

Ermintrude answered. Rain had said that she would stay; one place was as good as another, she said. No point in going anywhere. 'Auntie Myra, I don't know what to do with Rain. She just sits in her room all day, or sleeps.'

A few months later, Ermintrude wrote to say that Rain was working, that they had found her a job as a maid with a family in New York. Then she lost the job, or in fact she left the job. One day she just didn't go back, and didn't answer when Ermintrude asked her why. Ermintrude wrote to say that Rain just stayed at home, not bathing unless you told her to, hardly eating, and sometimes talking to herself. 'The two of us living together now, Auntie Myra. Daddy moved out. He and Rain never get along. They don't even talk to each other. I think Rain better go home, you know.'

Then Rain found another job, but didn't stay. 'Auntie Myra, when I start to quarrel with her, she asked me, "What is the point, Ermintrude? Where it leading? What we doing it for?" Auntie Myra, I don't know what to do.'

For a long time, Lyris and Myra had no news. Rain had been in Brooklyn for almost five years when there was news that she was in the psychiatric ward of a Brooklyn hospital. For the next eight years, Rain was in and out of hospitals, never seeming to adjust to life in Brooklyn, never doing the sewing she loved, working as a maid in the homes of various families. Then a letter from Ermintrude said that Rain had been placed in an insane asylum.

'I don't know what to do, Aunt Myra,' Ermintrude wrote. 'Is not that Rain is mad, really, but there is no-one to take care of her. She doesn't like Brooklyn. She is always shivering. Recently she got a job again working as a maid with a family, but they say she never does anything, and so she lost the job.

At home, she just sits down all of the time, and it is a problem. She doesn't eat, she won't bathe, or anything. Just stares and doesn't say anything.'

Myra said she should be sent home. 'Don't leave her in any New York asylum. Send her home.'

For weeks after Rain returned, she stayed with her aunt and cousin. Then Myra died suddenly of a heart attack. When Rain knew, she became hysterical. When Sister entered the house, someone said she was Orilie's daughter. It was the first time Rain was meeting Sister since her return. She started throwing everything in sight. Cups, plates, glasses, everything she could put her hands on was thrown in Sister's direction. She could not be calmed. The doctor committed her to the asylum in Paz.

The women walked back down the hill towards Paz, in time for the evening bus back to Victoria.

'A wasted life,' said Cousin Lyris. 'What a waste of a life!'

'Well,' Sister lifted her shoulders and opened her hands, palms upward. 'What to do! Rain too bitter. I never do Rain nothing in my life. What she and Mammie have, that is their business. I don't think I was even seven years yet when Rain leave this country, non, and Mammie never speak bad to me about Rain. Not really, except to say that she was rude, and all children does be rude.'

'She had to take care of you, and she wasn't happy in that house, to tell you the truth,' said Ermintrude. 'She had a hard life, a hard, hard life.'

'I don't think she have long to go again, non,' said Cousin Lyris. 'She light like a feather. She not in this world at all.'

'Rain take thing too much to heart,' said Sister again. 'Is not so people suppose to live. You can't take every little thing make you whole life so. Who could live like that!'

Tisane, on a visit from her first year of graduate studies at the University of the West Indies, had gone to visit her friend at the asylum. For the first time, the nurses saw some sign of life in this strange woman whose eyes had held them in thrall with their unspeakable sadness.

Rain smiled when her friend approached. 'I believe they think I'm mad, Tisane. They gave me shocks. They force me to eat through tubes.'

Tisane had resolved not to cry. She couldn't help it. The sobs just came. Rain touched her gently. Hugged her.

'Don't cry, Tisane. You never used to cry. I'm not mad. I just don't want to live.'

'I'm sorry, Rain. I shouldn't be crying like this. A real monkey.'

Rain smiled gently. 'No. That is Orilie. You forget?'

Tisane smiled through her tears. 'But what you doing here, Rain?'

'Well, I don't eat, I don't do anything for myself; so I can't stay by anybody. Besides, Auntie Myra dead, Cousin Lyris, sickly, Auntie Emma living in Orilie yard now and the sight of the house and Sister would make me go really mad!'

Rain laughed, touching her friend's hand. 'Don't feel sorry, Tisane. It don't have nowhere else for me to stay. I don't have to talk to anybody here. Here I could just stay sane watching people being mad, and wondering why.'

'You must get out of here, Rain. You can't live in the past. I always used to try to tell you it's no good to live on dreams, Rain. Face life, love.'

'Don't try to get me out, Tisane. This is the only place I sane, because everybody in here supposed to be mad; I like them; is the sane people I fraid. I happy here.'

Tisane's tears were threatening to fall again. Rain looked at her quizzically. 'People does grow up funny, in truth. You never used to cry before. Is either you getting wise, or you getting stupid.'

Tisane shook her head at her friend's attempts to make her laugh. *Rain* was comforting *her*. 'What happened in Brooklyn?'

Rain smiled, her eyes becoming remote. 'I'm a sunshine child, and I couldn't stand the rain.'

Tisane shook her head again. 'So you getting poetic!'

'How is university?'

The friends talked for hours. Tisane told Rain about her daughter. 'She's five. And Rain, she doesn't have a father.'

'She . . .?' Rain frowned, looking at her friend.

'No. Not Virgin Mary style or anything.' Tisane laughed. 'She doesn't have one who wants her. He didn't want to know. I've told her about it already. I'm not sure she quite understands yet, but she'll be able to deal with it. I'll see to that.'

'You not by any chance trying to give somebody a message?'

Tisane smiled. 'Not any message I haven't given before.'

Rain hugged her friend. 'Girl, you mother make you kind of all right. You not too bad at all, you know.'

Tisane wondered if she should tell Rain what she had named her daughter, but decided not to. Not yet. She would bring the child to visit her friend. She talked to her, though, about her last little brother, who had been born some time after Rain went away.

'He was really cute, Rain. He looked like Mammie. He was really mischievous and everything, too. We think he was poisoned.'

Rain said she had heard about this. She had heard someone say it may have been Mody's mangoes.

'Yes,' said Tisane, 'the doctors say it was "causes unknown". But that little boy was really writhing with pain and holding his stomach. Rain! I don't like to think about it. Mammie was really ill afterwards. I thought she was going to die too.'

Rain touched her friend's hand, and sat there not saying anything, just looking deep into Tisane's eyes as though she were trying to understand how one dealt with things like that. Tisane shook her head. That was always Rain's way, trying to understand so much that she forgot everything else. After a while, Tisane grinned. 'Life goes on, Rain,' she said.

Rain smiled. 'Tisane,' she said, 'you're my best, best friend in the world.'

Tisane knew she couldn't answer this without crying, so

she just hugged her friend, holding her close.

Afterwards the nurses talked to Tisane. This was the best they had seen Rain. What did Tisane think? But Tisane was non-committal. Rain had chosen her asylum, and would not want to be anywhere else. By the time Tisane was ready to leave, Rain had gradually withdrawn into her distant stare, and did not turn to say goodbye. Tisane saw her four more times before she left the island, but never again did Rain talk so freely.

The following year, when Tisane visited, Rain was in hospital, dying, they said, of tuberculosis probably picked up from the cold walls of the asylum. A sunshine child, thought Tisane.

Tisane visited Rain this time with her six-year-old daughter. Tisane was saddened at the sight of her friend. Rain's eyes were glazed, distant. She sat in her room with bowed shoulders, a tired old lady just thirty.

'Rain. Rain, you hearing me?'

Rain smiled, nodded.

'Rain, I want you to meet my daughter.'

The little girl moved forward, peeped up into Rain's face.

'Hello,' she said, touching the hands of this silent woman. 'Hello, my Mom says you have the same name as I do. My name's Rain. I'm six. What's your name?'

'Rain, my name's Rain.'

They looked into each other's eyes. 'Don't look so sad,' said young Rain.

Rain looked at Tisane. 'You know, Tisane, you're wonderful. I'm not sad any more, Rain. I'm all right now. Thank you, Tisane, I'm all right now.'

Rain lay back, closed her eyes. Tisane! she thought, Tisane! She wondered if Rain had been born on a rainy night, or on a day full of sunshine, perhaps. And then everything got mixed up in her mind, and she was remembering that day when her father had come and she had run away to Tisane in the trace. Tisane was putting her fingers to her lips and pulling her into the room. Any Rain would be all right with Tisane. Any

Rain. Tisane, bending over her friend, watching her lips
move, wondering if she were asleep, wasn't sure whether she
was muttering 'Rain' or 'Tisane'. She put her hand on her
friend's for a moment, and then tiptoed away with Rain.

The gravestone paid for by cousin Lyris, Tisane and
Ermintrude told a brief story:

RAIN DARLING

1929–1960

Gran

I want to tell you about my grandmother. Sometimes I don't like to think about Grannie because one night when I was in bed and thinking about her, one end of the bed went heavy, and it was just as if Grannie had just sat down there and the bed was sinking. I don't know. I don't know what happened, and then I fell asleep, but even in the morning I was afraid to uncover my head. And I still feel sure that that night Grannie was sitting on the edge of my bed, but I don't like to think about it.

Anyway, today it's not so bad. I won't get frightened. And the sun is shining, anyway. And nothing will happen because there are so many houses around. Too many houses. I like this little patch here where the sun is shining on this little bit of wall, and today is nice because it's like a holiday, and a lot of people are away. That's why Mom let us come outside to play. My brother is playing on the hill with his friend, running up and down the alley, so I can sit here and imagine things and tell stories for as long as I like, so that is nice. But I don't like it usually. I don't like living in town.

I don't like the small apartment. And there's no yard to play in. And sometimes the people living upstairs make a lot of noise. Mom says it was good to move in to the town for school and things, and now we can go to the cinema sometimes, and even walk down to the beach on a Sunday morning if we leave early before the sun gets too hot and go with money or take food or something. But I still liked it better when we lived in the country, where we had a big yard, and could shout, and laugh, and play cricket and things. We could even pick mangoes and sugar-apple and things.

Here, the moment you make a little noise, Mom says 'sh-h-h! There are people nearby.' Or even if you get licks from Mom, you can't bawl and make noise because other children will hear and laugh at you in school next day. No. I don't like living in town. No space. No space at all.

I think in a way that is why I remember Grannie so much. Because it was only after she died that we moved down to town. Mom would never have moved with Grannie. Grannie didn't like town *at all*! And anyway it was only *after* Grannie died that Mom and my stepfather, Uncle Delroy, decided to separate. But that is another story. Uncle Roy and Mom still see each other sometimes. Sometimes, he comes down for weekends, but he is so strict, I don't like it when he comes. And although I wish we still lived in the country, I'm glad that Uncle Delroy and Mom don't live together all the time again!

But anyway, let me tell you about my grandmother! About my grandmother, and Kairon's grandmother, too. Kairon is my brother. And Bevan. Uncle Delroy is their father, but he is not my father. But I'm not sorry. And even with Kairon and Bevan he is still very strict. He shouts at us all the time when he's here.

Kairon can be a real pest sometimes. He wants to know everything. If you have something and you don't show it to him, he will pull it away, even if it tears or falls down or something. Kairon! A real pest! He is ten, two years younger than me. Bevan is only little. Four years! He's cute! He's alseep now! We call him Ants-Man! Because he would sit for hours just staring at ants. Me and Kairon call him Ants-Man, but Mom says he's the ants-doctor. He could watch ants for *zonks*.

Bevan was Grannie's favourite. She didn't mind about Kairon, but she didn't like me *at all*! I didn't mind, really, because it used to be fun sometimes, just passing by her and watching her frown up her face. She used to tell me I look like my father like what! I don't think she liked my father. In fact, Mom says she didn't. But Daddy didn't mind and anyway he died when I was still a baby. He used to work digging a quarry and the stones fell down on him one day. Mom says the whole quarry caved in and he was buried alive. That sounds strange! Buried alive! It's creepy! Sometimes I don't believe he's really dead, and I imagine people coming with lanterns and masanto and things in the night and shouting to tell Mom that they found Mark Selby alive.

Once I told Mom this and she said, 'Nonsense!' I suppose it's nonsense in truth, because it's a whole twelve years almost. But Mom says they never found the body, because it was too deep, and they didn't have good enough equipment, and they found another man who was all broken and twisted up. But I still can't help it. Sometimes I feel is like my father not really dead. Is not as if they found a body! Anyway, Mom says it makes no sense living in Never-Never land. Makes no sense.

And about two years afterwards, Mom met the man. I mean, Uncle Roy. And I glad he not my father. Grannie didn't like him either. I don't see how *anybody* could like him, really, but Mom says a lot of ladies like him, because he nicer to other people than to us. And anyway sometimes all of a sudden he talks and laughs with us as if he is a nice person. If he was *always* like that, perhaps he would be nice. I don't know.

Listen! Listen! You hear that noise in the distance? The ringing? That is the Anglican church bell. It rings like that every hour. Listen! It's four o'clock. You know how I know it's the Anglican church bell? Because of what it sings. Mom says that church bell and the Presbyterian bell on the other hill always having a fight. So the Anglican church bell have the nicest song and while the Presbyterian bell goes gong! gong! one after the other, stopping after each one, the Anglican bell has a lot of singing gongs, so that it says,

I don't tell lies
Scotch bells tell lies

over and over again, until it drown out the Presbyterian bells.

Anyway, to tell you about Grannie. It's not that I didn't like Grannie; it's just that it was nice to tease her. And she was full of jokes; she used to say jokey things, especially when she was vex. But she didn't like girls. Mom says she always preferred boys. And she would be able to stand girls if they were nice and polite, but Mom says that I encourage people not to like me, because I could be so rude. I don't know. That is what Mom says. And anyway, I know I liked to tease Grannie. But she was jokes. Let me tell you about her.

Last year, Christmas Eve like tomorrow will be, Grannie was sick. So Mom called the doctor. The doctor drove quite from town right up to St David's to see Grannie, yes. He was a big, big and important doctor but he knew my Uncle William who is in England now. They used to study together when Uncle William was doing, was doing . . . I not sure what he was doing, but they used to study together. So Uncle William tell Mammie for anything, anything at all she must call his doctor friend. So the doctor arrive. He drive up in his car, right up in the yard! Well not right up, but almost! He couldn't go right up because of the stony road, so he park the car down by the mammie-apple tree and then walk up with his bag and his . . . his . . . the thing they does sound people with. And when the doctor sounding Grannie, she only saying, 'Leave me alone, take you hand away from me, you no-count good-for-nothing! Take you hand away.'

Mammie was feeling so shame! She keep saying, frowning up her face and looking as if she want to cry like, 'Behave youself, non, Mammie!' And Grannie look up into the doctor face and she ask, 'Who you is?' Is Annette son?' And when the doctor say yes, Grannie say, 'Well is Christmas Eve yes. After me, Annette is the best baker in the whole of this St David's area, yes. She hot up she oven yet?'

And this time now, Mammie was feeling more and more

un. . .uncom-fortable. She say to Grannie, 'Mammie, let the man do he work in peace, non.'

She say, raising up her hand like this, opening them up and looking at Grannie, 'Well Mammie! How you could think this is Annette son? Tell me! How you come by this idea? Eh? Leave the man let him do his work in peace, non!'

And Grannie just keep pointing her finger up and down, up and down in the doctor face. The whole time Kairon and I were looking through the crack in the door. And then was the big joke. Grannie say, to the *doctor*, you know, 'All-you young people nowadays never give a thought to nothing and nobody. Christmas Eve when for you to be helping Annette with the baking, look where you is idling with you hand on woman chest!' I tell you! That was jokes! Even Mammie laugh! She couldn't help it. But when she hear me and Kairon laughing, she come to the room door looking for us, but we saw her coming and run back into the other room until she went back inside of Grannie's room with the doctor. Then we came out again.

Afterwards Mom ask, 'She'll be all right you think, doctor?' I don't remember exactly everything that happened, but I know that the doctor gave Mom medicine for Grannie and he say he will see her again in the New Year. And then, just as he was going, he stand right in front of the bedroom door and he look back at Grannie and he say something like, 'My mother used to bake a lot indeed on Christmas Eve, Mrs Malcolm. Indeed. In those big, huge ovens that make the bread taste so special. Oh yes!' Grannie get quiet. She looked at the doctor like this, for a long, long time and then she say, 'So you know I am Mrs Malcolm! I will have you know, sir, Theodora Constance Malcolm, daughter of the late great Mrs . . . Mrs . . . Emelda Grenade.' Mrs Emelda Grenade, I think.

'Mrs Emelda Grenade, and Mr Grenade. And *Mister* Grenade,' she say. And Doctor say, 'Please to meet you, Ma'am. Please to meet you, Ma'am,' just as if he was just meeting her for the first time, and then he said, 'And now I'm afraid I must be leaving. Goodbye.' And Grannie say, you think me grandmother was easy? She was a case, yes. She tell the doctor, 'Don't fraid, son. Do what you have to do. Walk good, and go and help you mother, like a good boy.' This time, Mammie only looking like she want to show the doctor the door quick. After the doctor go away, Grannie sleep for a long, long time. Almost as long as the time when she sneak away and walk far, far away from here, right down to Westerhall.

I will tell you bout that, too. That is another story. If I try to finish talk about Grannie, today, I will never finish, but I will tell you the nice ones. That day, she leave about ten o'clock the morning. Was a morning with a lot of sun. No rain. Perhaps me and Kairon were playing in the back. Because that time we had a big, big yard. We didn't see her. Perhaps Ants-Man was sleeping. Perhaps Mammie was in the back cooking. I don't know. But for sure the man wasn't there. He was out doing his work, planting potato or something down in the land. So Grannie run away. Mammie say she must be walk and rest, walk and rest, until she reach Westerhall. I sure she probably sit down on stone and sing, and pick small bush by the roadside and things. I don't know for sure. Not for sure. But that is the kind of thing that I *know* Grannie would do. And she probably stop and talk to a lot of sheep, and cows, and goats and things tying by the roadside and inside of people land.

Grannie is like that. Sometimes if you walking with her she would stop and stare at a cow and ask, 'How now, Brown Cow?' And the cow would be just there munching and looking at her. And Grannie would put both hands behind her back and move her head . . . she was short, and not so fat, and she had a lot of white hair that Mom used to plait for her . . . and she would shake her head and ask the cow again, 'I say, "How now, Brown Cow!" ' And then sometimes the cow would just lift its head and look up into the sky and say 'Moo-oo-oo!' And then Grannie, is as if I could see her now, she would shake her head and turn away and say, 'Thank you. Thank you very much. It's good to know that you are doing fine.' And then she would walk away saying to herself, 'Animals better than a lot of people! When you talk to them they will answer you! When you want to talk, they will listen! Animals! Yes. Yes. The lowest of these have something to teach us! The lowest of these! Is we that low! Is we self that low!' And sometimes for the whole walk after that she would be talking to herself about animals and people.

And I remember once when that happen and me and Mammie were walking with her, I ran out in front of her and shout out, 'The lowest of these!' And perhaps I make a somersault or something in front of her. I can't remember exactly. And . . . yes, was a somersault. Because as I was standing on my head, I remember I hear her say, 'If I had a child like that, I hiding it away somewhere and I not letting nobody know that is mine! I tying it out in the pasture or something!' And I remember Mom laughed, and she told me, 'Yes. You get what you deserving. You so damn disgusting!'

But I didn't mind. Was jokes. Anyway, about Westerhall. Where I reach now? How I come to talk about animals and things? Oh yes! Although I can't say for sure what Grannie did while she was walking, I know the kind of thing that she would do.

So when she reach Westerhall now, in a place far, far away, down by the sea and not *so* far from St George's, she went into a shop. Mammie say she went in and ask for a glass of water or something. And as she was talking, people realise is not a lady from around there. So they asked her where she came from. So Grannie now was so tired, she ask them for a box. A box, a bench, anything, just so that she could sit down and rest. The people tell Mammie that Grannie said she come from a land far, far away; a land they call St David's. She tell them exactly where she come from, and about Mammie and Uncle Roy, and she said . . . Mammie say she tell them, 'In that St David's place the strangest of strange things happen. So I'm sailing, I'm sailing to find my fortune. Like the . . . the Duke of York, I think she say, with my ten thousand men. I'm marching to seek my fortune.' And when the people in the shop asked Grannie, 'Where are the men?' she said, 'They following behind.' And when I think of this story I always think, Suppose they had seen ten thousand men march in for true, what would those people in the shop do? But I told Mom that too, and she said that's nonsense *again*, because that would be bout all of the men in the whole of Grenada. Imagine! Not St David's, you know! *Grenada!* It makes me wonder if the Duke of York had ten thousand men in truth!

Anyway, while the people in the shop were there listening to all these jokes, they sent a message through the police station to tell us where Grannie was. So now Uncle Roy went all the way to Westerhall to find her. And because she just don't like him already, and Mammie had to stay with us, Miss Doris, Mammie friend, went with him. It's a good thing Miss Doris went, because they had to walk all the way back; it was too late even to get a bus or a lift with anything even if something would stop. They had to walk all that way, and because Grannie was tired, she was walking one today, one tomorrow; one today, one tomorrow; slow, slow, slow. And when Uncle Roy try to carry her on his back, Miss Doris say that Grannie say she rather sit down and make her peace with the Lord on the side of the road. Because is not only one home she have to reach, and if she could only reach one by riding on the back of some worthless man, she rather sit down by the side of the road and ride on the back of the Lord to her heavenly home. Mom and Uncle Roy laugh for days about that! You think I joking when I tell you that Grannie was something else?

So in the end Miss Doris carry her a little bit sometimes, and the two of them hold her hand and almost drag her sometimes. When they reach home here, Miss Doris was *carrying* her on her back. Fancy that! I never know Miss Doris was so strong. And by that time it was well late. About ten o'clock in the night. And when Mammie ask Grannie where she come from, Grannie was so tired that she couldn't even answer. In fact, before Mammie well finish asking the question, Grannie stretch out on her bed and she fell asleep right away. Right away. And she slept for a long, long time. Until the next day about two o'clock. Either twelve o'clock or two o'clock. I can't remember for sure, but it was well late the next day.

That is the end of that story. But I haven't told you the biggest story about Grannie yet, and is really because it's almost Christmas Eve and I remember *that* one that I start to talk about Grannie, so I *must* tell you that one.

Watch! You see those ants running around by my toes? If Ants-Man was here, you would just see him with his bottom in the air, and his two hands by his knees there. And he would be bending over and just staring at those ants. Sometimes I wonder what he is seeing. Sometimes we just stop and watch with him to see if we could see something too. And sometimes when we do that, he would stop and turn to us and start to explain something, moving up his hands as if he's explaining shapes, and as if he is asking us questions and explaining things. But none of us can understand what he is talking about. Sometimes Mom laughs and looks puzzled like, and she would say, 'Well, I don't understand this boy! What pleasure could he find in an ants' nest so? Well this is the strangest child!' And you see as now is Christmas and Mom will buy something for us, the only thing Ants-Man will like is a book with a lot of drawings of ants, or even other insects too but ants for sure in it, or Mom said that she would try to see if she could find a toy that is an ant. But yesterday I hear her saying is as if these toy people and them don't take a fancy to ants! So I don't think she find anything.

Anyway, last year Christmas . . . Wasn't last year Christman, non. Was this year. In January. Was one commotion. Grannie die on the eleventh of January. Mom say all the time she was there talking nonsense to the doctor, was death that was staring her in the face. You ever think of that? Death staring a person in the face? You ever think of what Death look like? I always wonder if Death was staring Grannie in the face in truth. And what she was seeing when she look at Death. In fact, what both of them was seeing. You ever wonder if Death is like a person? Mom say Death was staring her in the face!

Anyway, Grannie was eighty years old when she died. Nearly eighty-one! Mom say she don't think a lot of people live to be so strong at eighty! And Grannie was strong in truth! But just before she die she used to lie down a lot, and she used to say, 'Oh Lord! Me meat tired! All me meat hurting me, yes!' I didn't even used to laugh at that time, because I used to feel sorry for her, and she used to say a lot, 'Lord, if it be thy will, thy will be done!' And sometimes I even used to see Mom wiping the side of her eye, and she used to say, 'Nothing to say. Me mother well work a lot in she time already, yes. No wonder she could walk the streets of Grenada almost up to the end as if they belong to her. They belong to her in truth, yes. She work fixing road all over this country; in St David's, in Sauteurs, in Victoria, in Westerhall, in this very town here! All over the country! And you know, that was the first time I ever know that Grannie work on the road in Westerhall; is no wonder she could find the way to walk all down there; and Mammie say in those days they didn't have much transport; people either used to travel by donkey cart from wherever they living, or they used to walk.

So when Grannie lying down sick there, Mom say, 'She don't have nothing to show for it, but this country is hers for sure! If is not hers is nobody own! She body *must* be hurting her, yes, because all she strength in the cracks in the roads in this country. And when she wasn't walking fixing roads, she baking bread to sell and for us to eat.' And was as if Mom was getting sad and vex at the same time. And then she would just calm down and say like Grannie, 'Lord, if it be thy will, thy will be done!'

Anyway, after Grannie die, Mom say, 'Nothing to say! She satisfy the Lord and had years to spare!' And Auntie Aleantha, Mom sister who living in Sauteurs, was there the night Grannie died. I remember it so well. I don't like to think

about it, really, because I remember me and Kairon were
sitting in the dining room, and we were really, well, not
frightened, really, because Mom and Uncle Roy and Auntie
Aleantha and Miss Doris were there; and there was a lot of
light in the house. Me and Kairon were sitting in the
dining-room, and there were two lamps on the table; the big,
big lamp and a small lamp. And there was a small lamp in the
sitting room and the ordinary big lamp was in the big room.
And Mammie and Auntie Aleantha had a small lamp in the
sitting room where they were with Grannie. And then Uncle
Roy was sitting down outside in front of the kitchen door
with the lantern. So it had a lot of light about. And then again
was moonlight night. But all the same it was quiet and sad.
And everybody was either talking in a low, low voice or not
talking at all.

And then when it was late, late, Mom's uncle, Great Uncle
Son-Son, come into the yard. The dogs bark when he come
into the yard. And then Bingo start howling. And Auntie
Aleantha rush out of the room and she kind of whisper out
loud at Rover and Bingo, 'Hush! Hush you noise, there!' but I
think is Bingo she was really shouting at, because it was
howling, and that mean death. And then Kairon look at me,
well, he didn't look at me really, because he had his head
down, and his chin was on the table, and he had his hand
stretch out and he was turning a knife on the table over and
over, and then he say, 'Coral, you fraid?' And then I say,
'Yes, you?' And he shake his head, like, to tell me yes. And
then we hear Great Uncle Son-Son ask Uncle Roy, 'The old
lady going? I just get the message? She going?' And Uncle
Roy say, 'It look so, yes. It look so.' And next thing Great
Uncle Son-Son come inside and he pass through the dining-
room and he say soft, soft, 'Children,' and he touch me on
my head, because I was in the passage like, where he had to
pass to go through the sitting-room into Grannie's room.
And I answer so low that the voice didn't even come out. And
I'm sure it was the same thing for Kairon, because both of us
clear our throat same time after Uncle Son-Son pass through

the room.

Uncle Son-Son is Grannie uncle, you know. Imagine that! Is her uncle but he younger than her. Mom say that he was *her* grandmother's last brother, and he born after his big sister – that was our great grandmother – had Gran. Imagine that! But Uncle Son-Son not young, you know. He young to how Grannie was, but I see him the other day, and he looking as old as Grannie was looking just before she died. And he wasn't so before. He was stronger before. Is as if he get old all of a sudden. But I don't mean nothing, you know, about him dying or anything. Is just that he get a little bit older now.

Anyway, was only a little while after Uncle Son-Son go inside, I hear Mom start to cry like. You know, as if her mouth close and she crying. I will never forget that! Never! And Kairon sit up on his chair and his face go all funny! Is as if he *squinge* up himself and he stretching his hands down in front of him, and he biting his lips and licking his lips with his tongue, and then his eyes opened big, big. I don't know how *I* was looking, but maybe Kairon could tell you! I just know that I get up from my chair, and I went and sat down next to Kairon, and he moved over to give me room, and both of us put our heads down on the table and *squinge* up.

And then we feel somebody pass through the dining room, walking, and we thought was Auntie Aleantha from the way the person walking fast and soft, and was her in truth, because we hear her voice saying to Uncle Roy, 'It all over, yes. The old lady gone.' And Uncle Roy say something like, 'Well! She live out her years, eh!' And then we feel both of them pass back through the dining-room, but we still didn't look up.

And then we hear voices muttering inside as if they praying or something. The same sort of sound as when you saying the 'Our Father' over and over again. And then I start to say it in my mind too. And I don't know what happen again. Except that Bingo *and* Rover start to howl and howl and this time nobody didn't tell them to stop. And me and Kairon just sit down even closer together. And then we must have fallen asleep. I kind of remember as if somebody was carrying me.

And the next thing I know it was morning and Mom was waking up me and Kairon, and I realise that we were on the big bed in the room that was Mom's and Uncle Roy's.

And then Mom said, 'You grandmother died last night.' And Kairon and me didn't say anything. And then Mom said, 'The hearse coming for her in a few minutes; you want to come and look at her?' And both of us said, 'No,' same time. And Mom said, 'Nothing to be afraid of; she live her life out; she die peaceful in her bed when the Lord ready for her; God be praised.'

And Mom sat down on the bed there with us, and she looked kind of sad and far away. She looked up at the windows, as if she was looking outside at the plantain trees and the coconut trees, but she was really thinking far, far away, because she said, 'The one person she would've like to be there, eh! The apple of she eye! He disappear these donkey years in Maracaibo, nobody know where to find him!'

And we knew she was talking about Uncle Isaac. Because that was she and Auntie Aleantha only brother by their mother. They say he went to work in Maracaibo, in Venezuela, in the oilfields, a long, long time ago. And once somebody told Mom that they had seen him and gave her an address. But Mom said she tried to contact him and she think perhaps he didn't want to be in touch with anybody, because he never answer or anything. And then Mom said she heard that he wasn't doing too well, and perhaps he shame, but he have nothing to shame of, because from time poor people working hard and getting nothing for it, so not because you leave you own country and go in another one, thing does change. So is nothing to shame of. Is no fault of his. And then she write him again. But he still didn't answer. And Mom said, '*Zafè-i*. He always have nasty habit anyway. Never think bout nobody but himself. So *zafè*.' And up to this day, we never hear anything more about Uncle Isaac. And sometimes I wonder if is nasty habit in truth, or if Uncle Isaac just . . . well, just *can't* get in touch somehow.

Anyway, afterwards, they told everybody about the death

and the funeral and the wake and everything. All the cousins
and the friends and relatives and everybody. And they put it
on the radio, too. And when the announcement came over
the radio, our names were *there*. Six grandchildren, they said,
and they call out June and Janice for Auntie Aleantha, Oris,
nearly a big lady already; she leave school and everything,
Uncle Isaac child with a lady in Grenville before he disappear,
and then, big and broad, *Coral, Kairon and Bevan*, of St
George's. That was really exciting!

And Uncle Son-Son was the one who plan the *real* nice
part. He say to Mom, 'So Veda, Dora gone yes! Live full
four-score years on this earth and heading to start another one
when the Good Lord say . . . "Come on, now, step aside and
give somebody else a chance!" Who to fight with that? She do
well. She bat nearly a century. All of is going. Meself, I don't
have long again.' I remember that as good as ever. I does
think about it now when I see him. Because I remember
Mom telling him he have a good few years yet, and Uncle
Son-Son say, 'Perhaps. Perhaps not. I not worried. Next
month, meself, I hitting three-score and ten. I satisfy.' And he
even say whenever the Lord ready, somebody else could get a
chance to see what they could do. I wonder if I could *ever* talk
like that? I don't know. I feel I will just always fraid to die. I
don't know.

You hear that? You hear that noise and shouting going
down the alley? That is Kairon and his friend running there!
Mom will call him inside just now. In fact, she will call both
of us inside.

But to tell you the rest of it. Uncle Son-Son say that
Grannie must get a real proper burial. The full works. Not
like in a modern-day vroop vrap! Just so he say. No vroop
vrap! If a person live so long and do so much, he say, you
suppose to give them a proper send-off.

And then one day, must have been two nights or three
nights afterwards, I can't remember. They bury Grannie right
away two days after she died, and I think it was the night after
the funeral, was still moonlight, everybody gather, and thing

start.

People hugging each other and saying, 'So Dora gone, yes! Dora gone!' Some crying, some just kind of shaking their heads and making sounds in their throats and saying, 'Oh yes! After one time is another, eh!', and, 'Praise the Lord! She bat well, nothing to say!' and things like that. Oh yes! And something I remember. Somebody say, 'Man does only *think* he brave when God playing Zaè, playing he sleeping let man form he fashion. But when he say you out, what to do? You can't say was the pads and not the wicket. You out!' Me and Kairon did really like that. Was the first time we start to think of God as a bowler. You know? I like that. You could imagine God running up like Sobers or Gibbs or . . . or Ramadeen who Daddy used to talk about? I did really like that.

Anyway, that night they talked a lot about Gran. They say that Dora died in January, proper time, right after Christmas, when normally she settle she business and all the baking done. They say that Gran used to bake sometimes for all the people around. People all up in Hope used to buy her bread, and down in the cocoa under the Grand Bacolet Great House, and even up among the Indian people in Kumar, right up to Kumar junction.

They say people used to bake on Christmas Eve in the moonlight. And even self they don't have moonlight, *chou poule*! Uncle Son–Son say, 'Masanto makin fou-fou until bread bake!' And to besides, he say, people making moonlight with their mouth and their talk.

That was really a nice night, you know. Me and Kairon hear so many stories we get drunk and sleepy with stories. And all the time Grannie living I never knew so much about her. Is only that night of the wake that I understand what she and the doctor were talking about the night they talked about the oven outside.

Uncle Son–Son and Mom say that for baking, the oven was outside. Outside in the yard. A big, tall oven made of bricks and stones and mortar. And Uncle Son–Son say is not *fou-fou* mortar mix like in nowadays mortar mix. He say that these vroop vrap days people does mix mortar like joke. They do everything like joke. Like is just for today and not for tomorrow. In the long-ago days, they used to mix mortar with something they called white lime. *That* was the proper thing for the oven.

And they had to build the oven high, right up on a level with a person's face, so that they could watch into it. And it had a mouth at the front. They said a mouth, but it sound to me as if it was like a kind of door.

And Grannie used to stand up in front of her oven in her yard in St David's with a long stick in her hand when she was baking. A long stick with a flat part. Like . . . like . . . I can't see anything around here to show like what, but when we used to live in St David's, Uncle Son-Son showed me a flat piece of board in the yard, and he put a sort of handle with it, to show me what it used to look like. And they used to call it a peel, or something like that. And they used to make it long because the oven had to be hot, hot, so Grannie had to stand far away from it. And Mom say that is where they get the habit of bathing before and not after they bake from, because after you face this fire, you body too hot to go and dip into cold water right away. And was even the same with ironing, because they didn't want to bathe after facing a coalpot of hot coals.

And is only since then I understand why Mammie stop so. Because even now sometimes, if she make me press a little blouse or something with the *electric iron*, you know, and I go and bathe afterwards, she shouting at me! You believe that?

Anyway, I was telling you about the oven and how Grannie used to bake. Mom and Auntie Aleantha used to help her. The two of them used to stand up on the side and put the bread on the flat part of the peel when Grannie hold it out and say 'Bread!' or, 'Ready!' or, 'Now!' or something, you know, to let them know it was time. And then after Grannie put in enough bread and the oven was full, she used to go up nearby and close the oven door quick, quick.

This time now, Mom and Auntie Aleantha squeezing out water from cloth in a bucket, squeezing it, squeezing it until the heavy water come out, and then they handing the cloths to Grannie. She used to take them and fit them in all around the oven door, making sure to close up any cracks, so that the heat would stay in. I'm not sure why they used to *wet* the cloths, but perhaps it was because the oven was so hot, and the cloth would burn up if they didn't wet it. I don't know for sure.

But I forgot to tell you something. I'd better hurry up. You hear the church bell? It only do 'I don't tell lies' so it is quarter past something, must be quarter past five, and Mom sure to call out soon to ask me to come inside and do something. I forgot . . . come to think of it, I forgot a lot!

Anyway, let me tell you fast! They used to burn a lot, a lot of wood inside the oven to make it hot. And then Grannie would know when it was hot enough. If she peeped inside of the oven and said, 'It not ready yet, non,' then they would have to put in another bundle. And Mom says they did that until the roof of the oven was white hot. And then they would take a long broom . . . a stick with blacksage bush tied on to the end, and sweep it out.

The other thing I forgot to talk about was the hole at the side. Because they couldn't sweep out all of this hot ashes in front where Grannie had to stand up. So there was this hole which they called an ash-hole. I really like that word; but when Mammie tell us about it and I juk Kairon for us to laugh, she give us one bad-eye! And she say 'Nowadays all word spoil; youall little devil doesn't have nothing good in you head.' Anyway, the ash-hole was on one side of the oven, usually on the left side when you facing the oven, I think, from what Uncle Son-Son say, and that's where they used to sweep all the ashes through. All the old coal and the ashes and everything.

And then at the end of all this, when you see . . . Oh yes! And I forget to say that when all of this going on, especially on a day like Christmas Eve, it would have a lot of people around, some waiting for the oven to be free if they don't have one in their own yard to do their baking, some just around talking and laughing and drinking rum and telling stories and thing. And to put the bread inside the oven, they used to put it down on leaves, bluggoe leaf, or balishae leaf; each bread on a long strip; a long strip below, and a long strip covering it.

And then while it baking and they waiting is when they telling stories and talking all things; everybody business, all jokes that happen in the area and everything. And then when Grannie say, 'Open up, let's see if it ready!' Mom and Auntie Aleantha used to scramble to move the long stick from behind the heavy board that used to keep the oven door close. You know, is the strangest thing, sometimes I try to imagine Mom with she dress, and the dress band hanging perhaps or something and she little plaits and thing, running and helping Grannie baking, and the idea does just make me laugh. I can't inagine it at all! Once I ask Kairon to draw what he think it look like, because he's good at art and I can't do it at all, but he never did it. I wish I could draw! Because I'm sure I would get an idea, just from trying to do it.

Once I asked Mom if she had a picture of herself when she was a little girl, and she just sucked her teeth and asked me if I think those days were days like today, when 'camera knocking dog all over the place.'

Anyway, if the bread wasn't ready, Grannie might say something like, 'It could take a little browning below still,' so they might turn it over or something.

And then, when the bread came out, was time for the tart, the coconut tart – up to now nobody could make coconut tart like Mom! Nobody! – the coconut tart, and they used to put that to bake on a flat tin, and the cake and potato pudding and the roast meat and thing!

Look! Mom ain't call me yet; she must be well busy when you see that; but I getting well hungry talking about all this thing, so let me go inside.

But just to tell you that after everything done, now,

somebody else might want to come and use the oven. And sometimes the baking going on until Christmas morning, and people telling their story and thing. Sometimes Grannie staying and listen and talk, sometimes she going inside and put up curtains or throw herself down on the bed to rest or something.

And Mom say even that time, too, she used to say things like, 'All me meat tired. Me hand tired, me foot tired, me head tired. Me leg tired! O god, ah tired!' And she always used to say, even up to the time we know her, she used to say, 'Look, let me go and put sleep to bed, eh!' And during the wake Uncle Son-Son keep on saying 'Dora, eh! Theodora! This time she put sleep to bed for good!'

'Yes, Mom? No, Mom. Is me alone. I just sitting here telling stories. Kairon in the alley with Allan. Yes Mom. I was just coming, yes.' You see what I tell you. I knew she would call me. She was baking for Christmas and sewing and thing. She say I so damn lazy that she don't have patience to teach. She rather do the thing herself. Me? I don't mind at all. And Kairon . . . Oh! He smart. Look him now! Coming driving with his mouth! She well leave us long. Hear the church bell! Must be quarter to! Perhaps after we eat, Kairon might remember something about the prayer part of what they do for Grannie. Because was praying, too, you know. Wasn't only telling story.

'Kairon! Come and hear something! You remember the time with Grannie? I was telling story. You remember the praise?'

'Praise?'

'Is praise or is prayers?'

'Dunno. Must be same difference. But I remember, yes. After we wash and dry the dishes, we will go back outside and tell story, right?'

'Mom won't let us go outside. You know that!'

'Will be moonlight, Coral!'

'You think you in St David's or what? Town moonlight on electric pole, yes. You know Mom doesn't let us go outside

down here.'
    'Okay. Well we will sit down in the room, then.'
    'Ants–Man still sleeping, you know, Kairon.'
    'Or in the drawing-room or somewhere.'
    'If Mom don't have something doing.'
    'Steupes. If we can't do it, we just don't do it. That is why I
don't like town, you know! If is in St David's now, we just sit
down in front of the door on the step!'
    'Same thing I say. Town really funny!'
    'Let's dry up the dishes fast, anyway, just in case!'
    It look as if Mom will go into her room and sew curtains.
Great! So we could stay out there in the living room, just
behind the dining table! So if we do this quick . . .

'You remember, Coral?'
    'You tell it. I was remembering and telling story all
evening. You tell this part.'
    'What part you tell?'
    'Everything that they were saying about how Grannie used
to bake and everything.'
    'That was before everybody reach and the prayers start.'
    'So you tell the prayers part.'
    'They get a lady from the Catholic church to pass the
chaplet. Even though Grannie was an Anglican. Mom say
Catholic people know good prayers and chaplet. And everybody was singing,

> One Our Father
> Ten Haily Marys
> For the souls in Pur-ga-to-ry!

> One Our Father
> Ten Haily Marys
> For the souls in Pur-ga-to-ry!

And then they had another song. In patwa. I not sure I
remember it exactly, but . . .'

'Start it. And I will sing with you.'

> *E las Bon Jé*
> *Mwen pwan trop tard*
> *Pèrdoné mwen*
> *Mwen ja perdi*
>
> *Tem mwen té la santé*
> *Tem mwen té bien iwé*
> *Mwen ba té shoinjé*
> *Si Bon Jé té la.*

'We well remember it. I don't know if we sing it exactly like them, but the Catholic people does sing it nice, nice. In fact, it wasn't only the Catholic people, because everybody, all the old people, know prayers songs. But the Catholic chaplet lady lead and after chaplet pass now, and all the *first* singing go, the real fête start. The chaplet lady leave early, I think.'

'Yes. She leave early, after she pass the chaplet and the fête start.'

'They pass coffee, they pass sandwiches, they pass cocoa and things like that. It was nice, but when the *real* rum-drinking start and people start to get drunk and stagger and thing, I hear Mom telling aunt – Auntie Aleantha – who was there too, that Grannic always used to say that this part of prayers is like "abusing prayers in a rum party". That sound just like Grannie. She wasn't easy, you know. You talk about that, Coral? You talk about Grannie?'

'Yes. I talk about Grannie.'

'And the rum drinkers start to sing all kind of songs. They had a nice one that go . . .'

'We better don't sing it too loud, eh, before Mom send us to bed.'

'All right.'

> *Mister Chairman, bring the rum come*
> *Mister Chairman*
> *If it's a quarter*
> *It's better than water*
> *Bring it with a willing mind*
> *If it's a quarter*
> *It's better than water*
> *Bring it with a willing mind!*

'That was jokes, yes.'

'And then right in the end, now, they get sad, sad again, and start to sing all kinds of hymns. It was really sad in the end. And the last thing I remember was Mom, Auntie Aleantha and Uncle Son-Son sit down on the sofa, and Uncle Son-Son had his arm round both of them, and Mom was crying, and Auntie Aleantha wiping her eyes, and everybody singing "Abide with Me". And Uncle Son-Son say, "Well, let us don't cry, eh! Bear up! Bear up! Is a proper farewell for Theodora Grenade, deceased, nothing to say. She live a full life, God be praised. She come with nothing. She work all she life and still she go with nothing." '

'Yes. And he say, "Lewwe pass one for Dora, eh, lewwe pass one for Dora and the years she make." Gluck. Gluck. They drink that. And they say, "She swim well against the current; nothing to say, she swim well." And then Uncle Son-Son say, "Lewwe pass another one for the whole Grenade generation and for the younger generation especially. Is up to them. Lewwe take one on their head." You remember that, Kairon? You remember when he say that?'

'I remember, yes. Ent I was there like you?'

'I just ask you if you remember. Nothing to get vex about.'

'Who getting vex? Look by the door. Watch!'

'What? Ants-Man? You wake up? Everybody going to bed just now, you self waking up? Come, come. Don't cry. We will sing for you.'

Tem mwen té ja sanché
Tem mwen té bien iwé
Mwen ba té konnèt
Ki moun ki la

Pèrdoné mwen
Mwen ba té shoinjé
Pèrdoné mwen
Mwen ba té konnèt

Madelene

'I don't want to be ungrateful,' said Madelene, lowering herself on to the sofa. Corinne looked up from filing her nails. She opened her mouth to say something. Thought better of it. Her aunt, she decided, wasn't really talking to her. Madelene moved her hand across the cushion. This was her favourite seat. Her favourite bed, too. Sometimes, at night, she would just relax there and go to sleep instead of bothering to go into the room. These days I don't even like to go to sleep! she thought. I don't like nights. It's not like resting. It's like waiting. Madelene sighed. Corinne glanced up and quickly moved her eyes back to her nails, because her aunt was looking at the photograph above her head.

When I sleep in this room, Madelene was thinking, I'm closer to her. I can't say it's why I spent the money to buy this sofa, because I really needed something decent in here anyway. Friends and relatives and everybody always passing through New York on their way to somewhere and want a night rest. Anyway, I needed a sofa. But when I sleep out here, it just so happen that I'm closer to her.

Belle, her daughter, the one child God had seen fit to give her on this earth, had had her great grandmother Belle's eyes. But she had looked more like her grandmother, Ma Janie, with those big, thick, long plaits. The one child God had seen fit to give her on this earth.

'You calling you daughter *Belle*?' her sister, Corinne's mother, had asked her. 'All the trouble Grannie Belle make you see, you will take your good, good child and call after her?' And Madge had looked at her with something like admiration. 'Sister,' she said. 'If you don't find a place in heaven, it have no justice in this world.' And Madge, as usual, had challenged fate by adding, 'because if was *that* I had to do to secure *my* place in heaven, I would have lost out. Not me, sese! I couldn't call me good, good child after Grandma Belle.'

'Madge,' Madelene had told her gently, 'don't say things like that. You mustn't speak like that of the dead. Grannie Belle wasn't bad, really; she was just disagreeable because she was sick. That was all.'

'Is all right, Madelene. *You* are the one who mustn't speak badly of the dead. And nobody have to tell you that. Is a known fact that you wouldn't do it. You don't speak bad bout people when they alive, much less when they dead. Me? If Grandma Belle listening now, God rest the soul of the dead and all that, she know well is something I would say right to she face. So is all right. I treat her same way alive and dead. Just as she treat me all the days of me life that I could remember whether she was sick or she was well. No problem.'

Madge had been like that. Blunt, straightforward. And people liked her. They knew where they were with her. They would go to cry on Madelene's shoulder, but they didn't go to Madge if they wanted to have a good cry. They went if they were crying and wanted somebody to tell them to stop playing the fool, and why. Madge was like that, except when *her* tears started, and then because she had always been so strong with everybody, the only person she could lean on was Ancil. And Ancil didn't want anybody leaning on him. That was one reason he had liked Madge in the first place. Because she was so tough. Nobody could hurt her.

Madelene ran her hands along the cushions again and looked around the room. She had no picture of Madge on the wall. She couldn't bear that. All Madge's photos were of a woman who held her head high and had determination and fire in her eyes. A strong face. Thin, almost cruel lips. Only in some of them the eyes took over. And you could see the softness, the love. But in none of them was there the broken, silent woman that Madge had become before she died. Having a photo of Madge on the wall would somehow be a frightening thing.

It was after Madge died that Madelene had developed her fear of heights. Any heights. Even looking out from the window onto the steps below when someone rang the doorbell made her giddy now. And when she was in a car going along a bridge, she had to close her eyes. She couldn't look down at the traffic below without feeling ill and panicky and wanting to scream. Madelene closed her eyes now and thought about it. It's as if it is dangerous just to hold your head high. That couldn't be true. No. She couldn't keep a photo of Madge in the house. That is why it had been so painful and frightening bringing up Corinne and watching her grow into her mother.

Madelene looked at her niece, at the high cheekbones, at the two plaits circling her head, at the determination in the chin, at the scornful tilt of the lips. She closed her eyes. Please God! Please!

The ticking of the clock on top of the television pushed against her eyelids, making them jump nervously. Some days you could watch that clock and not hear a sound. And some days it talked so loudly that you could hear every syllable. Like today.

Madelene opened her eyes and looked around the room. At the refrigerator, the dining table, her shelves full of knick-knacks, the 1987 almanac on the wall. The television. Her photograph of Belle. And, opposite her, Corinne's face intent now on the page of the book she was reading. Thirty-seven years of life in New York crammed into four rooms in this apartment. This place was home, more home to her now than that hill in Grenada just over the sea. Now that she had stopped working, she actually missed the early morning trek to the corner of Church and Utica to get the bus. Walking with sleep still in her eyes, sometimes, but then by the time she was walking down the steps into Utica Avenue station, she was always awake. Awake and looking over her shoulder to see who was behind her. You didn't walk sleeping into the train station. No. Perhaps she didn't really *miss* that daily trek to work in the people's kitchen in Queens! You couldn't miss a thing like that. But it felt empty, still, getting up at five in the morning, and then realising you didn't have to start getting ready for work.

'I don't want to be ungrateful in truth, non, Lord! I don't want to be ungrateful. I have a good life. I don't want to be greedy either.'

Corinne looked up again. And this time Madelene's eyes met hers. Madelene chuckled. 'What?' she asked. 'What you looking at me like that for?'

'I don't know why I bother to come and sit with you, you know. When I'm here, you talk to the Lord, you talk to everyone you have secreted away in your memory, and you ignore me completely!'

'Oh come on, Corinne! You know that's not true.'

'Oh no? What's this you're saying about being ungrateful and being greedy?'

Madelene chuckled again. Leaned forward, stretching her arms along her legs, and when she looked up again, Corinne knew from the smile on her lips that she was going to say something her niece would have to unravel. Corinne sighed.

'It's all right, Auntie Madelene. I think I'd better read.'

'You see? Now I want to talk to you, you don't want to keep me company at all.'

Corinne closed her book. 'Shoot!'

'Don't tell me any shoot! I don't carry a gun.'

'All right, madam,' Corinne stretched, laughing. 'Tell me.'

'It's a story.'

'I guessed as much.'

'About a greedy, greedy man.'

'Oh! At least it have something to do with the way your thoughts have been going.'

'Is nothing to do with me. It's about Konpè Macucu.'
Corinne yawned.

'You see the same thing. You young people born in this country . . .'

'I'm just teasing you, Auntie Madelene. Tell me.'

'Once upon a time, Konpè Zaè, Konpè Macucu, and Konpè Tigre decide to make a big cook one day. They do all the work together, they fish, they hunt, and they go and dig a whole heap of potato and yam, they cut bananas, they knead their flour and make dumplin, and they cook a whole heap of food.

'When food ready, Zaè and Tigre watch one another and say, "The food plenty yes. It should have enough for all of us to eat, but just in case, we better get some more." Konpè Zaè say, "For how I know I hungry there, I really think we need some more food." '

Corinne chuckled. Madelene smiled at her niece. 'It have people so in truth, you know. Never satisfy. Anyway, Macucu say, "Me, I well tired. I not going any place now. Is just eat I waiting to eat." So Tigre decide he will go with Zaè to look for more crayfish under the river stone.'

'Well I think they were really stupid and greedy. I could see where that story is going already, Auntie Madelene.'

'That is the problem. But perhaps you only *believe* you see. Suppose you think you seeing and you not really seeing!'

Corinne clasped her hands lightly in front of her and looked with more attention at her aunt. Her stories were always like a test. Leaving you unravelling and unravelling. 'I'm listening.'

'Zaè and Tigre set out to get more crayfish. They sit down by the river stone, bend down, push in they hand, grabbing wind and water, wind and water. Whole time their belly grumbling and they thinking of the food they cook already. But they thinking how a few more crayfish would really liven up the taste. So they persevering. Wind and water. Wind and water.

'Macucu, meanwhile, back home, he watching the food

and he waiting. He watching the food and he waiting.'

'But he was really stupid. They left on such a foolish mission; he shouldn't even think about them!'

'Well, he watching and waiting. He know that their work inside the pot too, so he scratching his head, he watching and he waiting. He scratching his chin, he watching and he waiting.

'Down by the river, no luck. Wind and water. Wind and water. Macucu find, well, he waiting too long.'

Corinne's eyes narrowed. She watched her aunt's face.

'At last Macucu decide, "I will eat a little, little piece on the edge here. Right here. Just a little piece." '

Corinne relaxed. Chuckled again. 'Of course. The others too greedy!'

'Macucu say, "Oh God, hungry killing me. Let me take another little piece." So he bite piece of dumplin, drink a little bit of soup, eat piece of fish, dig into a little chunk of yam . . . and whole time he watching the road. No Zaè. No Tigre.'

Corinne laughed out loud. 'Wind and water,' she said, 'wind and water. That is all they will get!'

'Before Macucu well realise it, he finish the *whole* pot of food!'

'The man was hungry, Auntie Madelene! With reason!'

'When Tigre and Zaè reach back, tired, they ain't hold no crayfish, pot empty. Tigre look in; food say, "If you see me, take me." Zaè look in, he look around; he look up, he look down. He say, "Non. Well something funny. I could swear we leave a pot here, that was full of food. Somebody if I wrong, tell me I wrong." '

'He wasn't wrong at all. He was just too damn greedy!'

'So Zaè look at Macucu belly how it nearly touching the other partition in the corner over by you there, Corinne . . .'

'No, Auntie Madelene, that is too much!' Corinne looked back at the partition, thumped it, made a show of trying to pull her chair closer to Aunt Madelene's. 'Not over *here.*'

'And Zaè say, "Tigre, oh! You know, boy? I think I see the food." And before Macucu could move, because he so heavy he can't run at all, Zaè grab hold of him, and he tell Tigre to hold him on the other side. All how Macucu plead that he didn't do anything, they hold on to him. And Zaè look up into the sky quite over where the moon was shining she face nice, nice, and Zaè call, "Konpè Gigi! Konpè Gigi!" '

'Gigi is a bird?'

'Yes, Chicken-hawk! "Konpè Gigi!" So Gigi flap up he wings and he coming down to hear what happen. And Konpè Zaè say, "Konpè Gigi, do something for us. *Vini. Vini pwan Konpè Macucu épi alé, alé, alé jis soley ba épi lagé-y la sou plat woch sa-a!*" Okay! Okay! I will explain! I know you wouldn't understand that where you born in this Brooklyn here. He say, "Come, come, come and take Konpè Macucu; go with him, go far, far away, like where you see the sun going down far over there. When you reach right up there, just let him go, let him go, let him fall on this flat stone right here!" '

'Oh gosh! Auntie Madelene, where do you get these stories from?'

'But is who really greedy? So anyway Gigi take up Macucu in his claws and he going up. And when he reach far, far up, he look back and he ask, "Here?" and Zaè and Tigre say, "No. *Alé, alé, alé.* Go, go, go!" He travel, he travel, he travel, he stop again and he ask, "Here?" And they say, "No. *Alé. Alé.*" '

Corinne grinned, repeated a patwa word she had heard her aunt say in similar circumstances, '*Tonnè!*'

'*Tonnè* is right! At last Gigi reach quite where they can't even see him, and he up there close to the sun in the sky. They hearing the voice from far, far away asking "He-e-e-re?" And Zaè and Tigre shout back. "*Oui!* Ye-e-e-s!" And Gigi shout out "Now!"

'And they wait! And they wait! And they wait! Zaè watching the sky. Tigre watching the stone! Zaè watching the sky! Tigre watching the stone! They wait! But was a long way up Gigi went. So they wait for about – almost two hours!'

'Auntie Madelene!'

'How I buy it, so I sell it. I make no profit. But then all of a sudden Zaè see this big barrel figure come flying through the sky and before he could look down good Tigre say, "Woy!" '

Madelene looked down at the carpet, at the lone bedroom slipper which had suddenly become a stone waiting for Macucu's body. Corinne looked, pulled her lips apart in a grimace, drew her feet closer to her, and said, 'Yuk!'

'Child, you should see that stone! You should have seen that stone! I tell you! Konpè Macucu belly open up from up here, right under his chest, go right down.'

Corinne turned her head away, towards the blank face of the television. Closed her eyes. Opened them and turned back towards Auntie Madelene.

'Split! Burst wide open on the flat stone. Crayfish come out. Chicken come out. Callaloo come out. Dumplin come out. Yam come out. All the waters come out! Everything just mix up, mix up.'

'Auntie Madelene! How disgusting!'

'Chile, I tell you! Zaè watch and he shake his head. Tigre watch and he hold on to his belly as if he fraid it fall open too. What the two of them do with what come out is another story. But child you ever see? A nice, strong young man like Macucu, look where he end up through greedy! Look where he end up! His close, close friends give up on him!'

'But they were the greedy ones in the first place!'

'You telling me it have *degrees* of greedy? Who to judge? But me? Thirty-seven years in New York! Thirty-seven years! Child, I don't want to be greedy, I don't want to be ungrateful to the Lord for the little he let me put by. Who is to say? Who is to know?'

Corinne wasn't sure what to feel. She was torn between wondering what in fact the two had done with all that came out of Macucu's belly and trying to figure out the whole story. Madelene put her head back against the cushion and closed her eyes. Corinne ran her hands along the mahogany arms of the chair on which she sat. Thirty-seven years in New York, ending up not so far from where you start, and talking about not wanting to be greedy! Corinne sighed.

What was it that made some people feel rich when they had so little and some people want so much?

Corinne wished she knew more about her relatives. Aunt Madelene was the only one, really. 'Heaven will be a place full of surprises,' Aunt Madelene always told her. And Corinne had once said to her, 'The biggest surprise will be the existence of heaven itself!' Aunt Madelene had looked at her strangely. 'That is modern talk,' she had said, 'but for you it not so modern. It sound like you mother anyway. She would say things like that from time. From time.'

Once, Corinne couldn't understand the stories about her mother. She couldn't understand how a woman whom people said had been so strong and so full of life could have lost interest in life and literally drunk herself to death because her husband had walked out on her. Then, two years ago, at thirty-two, just when she thought that she would always be in control and *she* would decide what relationship she wanted and didn't want, she had found herself in the middle of a relationship which she just hadn't known how to handle. Corinne had begun then to understand. Had begun to understand and become so angry with the pain of understanding and drinking and smoking that she talked herself out of madness.

There were times that she had been tempted to talk to Auntie Madelene. But she would rush home from work and begin to cry the moment the door of the apartment closed behind her. Once, after she moved to her own place and had to tackle not just a few narrow stairs but the lift, the tears had actually started in the lift. She had just kept staring at the number 6, right in front of her eyes, until the door of the lift opened, releasing her. Thank heavens the two pairs of eyes which had shared the lift with her had been focused inside themselves, on their own affairs. Those weeks of making sure that she had rum, whisky, beer, anything, so that she could drink herself to sleep! She never smoked in the apartment. She couldn't stand the smell. But she did, on the platform, waiting for trains, when the sight of people sleeping in the corners had made her weepy in a way that it hadn't really before. Well, it had, but she had been able to control it. Would talk about all of that with . . . with . . . him and felt different then. And then, perhaps it had been a television programme, or her friends talking, or her own distaste for smoking, or all of those, that had made her ask herself first of all whether it was worth it smoking herself to death because of some man. It was more the answer than the question that had frightened her. Because she had told herself that she wasn't interested really in whether she lived or died. And then had said, loudly, on the train platform, 'Bullshit!'

No-one had turned to look at her, of course. Two youths standing near her were swaying and dipping to the sounds from their earphones. A woman was looking worriedly at her watch. 'Rubbish!' Corinne had said, then puffed thoughtfully again at the cigarette and eventually crushed it. It hadn't been the last, but it had been a beginning. What would Auntie Madelene say if she knew it all? Corinne knew for sure that she wouldn't let it happen again. She was learning, now, to value herself more. Although the damn stupid thing was that she had thought she knew that ages ago! But she knew now how it could have happened to her mother. Sometimes she thought that Auntie Madelene had guessed about her. But Corinne never told her. She couldn't tell her.

So when things were really going bad, she had speeded up her plans for going independent and found her own apartment. Needed her own space, she said. She would visit often. Auntie Madelene, of course, hadn't minded. Corinne had only continued sharing the apartment all of these years anyway because she knew that Madelene wanted the company. 'I will miss you, child,' Madelene had said, 'but you have to find your own way.' And so she had never seen the packets of cigarettes, the bottles of rum, and whisky, and gin. So stupid! So damned stupid! Poor mother! So possible!

Corinne looked at her aunt's face, at the lines curving around the sides and over her mouth, at the small, slim hands, loosely linked now below her stomach. Aunt Madelene, she knew, was afraid of death. And she thought that she was dying. There was something wrong, Corinne knew, but she wasn't sure what. Something wrong inside under her stomach just where the hands were clasped. Madelene knew, she felt, but didn't say. And this scared Corinne. She thought perhaps her aunt had some terminal illness; that she was keeping it a secret so that she would not worry anyone; she would carry all of the worry herself.

Madelene was muttering something as she dozed. Corinne stood up and bent over her. Moved away and sat down again. Looked up at the photograph of Belle. In the photo, Belle was about four years old. Four and a half, really. Auntie Madelene could say how many months, how many days after four. She had been buried in the cemetery here in Brooklyn thirty years ago. Auntie Madelene was always amazed because here in the cold, dark pain of Brooklyn all those years ago she had actually managed to find a cemetery called 'Evergreen'. Auntie Madelene always said that she wanted to be buried there too. Here in New York, which had become home, bad as it was, she said. Who to say where is home? Over there was home once, but . . . And Auntie Madelene usually shrugged at this point and said, 'Bad is bad wherever it is! Wherever it is! Trouble is always trouble! It might feel little better here because everybody little better off, but watch who at the bottom of the barrel! Just watch!'

Sometimes Corinne wondered whether Auntie Madelene really meant that. Or if she was just telling herself that because New York *had*, like it or not in a way, become her home. Corinne remembered the day when someone had actually tried to snatch her purse one early morning. As luck would have it, she was then walking with her cousin, who had come from Grenada hoping to stay. Corinne smiled. That was just plain bad luck! It was the first time Auntie Madelene had been attacked in the street. Cousin . . . Cousin . . . What was her name again? I don't even remember. Her karma was just bad, I suppose! Corinne chuckled. It wasn't a

joke, really, but that had confirmed Cousin . . . oh, Madonna! . . . that had confirmed cousin Madonna's worst fears
about New York and, even though they hadn't really lost
anything, because Auntie Madelene had shouted and cursed
the guy! Imagine! The poor guy, not expecting to hear such
words and get such a vigorous defence from a woman that
age, perhaps, had run off. Corinne smiled and looked at her
aunt's face, as gentle in repose as it was when alive and
questioning. 'We lucky he was just a novice,' Madelene had
said when recounting the story. 'He didn't ready yet. He only
think he want to thief!' Even though he hadn't taken the bag
that he was after, Cousin Madonna had booked her return
ticket the following week.

Madelene opened her eyes. Moved her fingers along the
base of her stomach. 'Sixty-seven is a good old age, yes, a
good old age,' she said without preamble. She looked at
Corinne, chuckled.

'What now?'

'I was remembering my husband,' she giggled. 'Your
mother used to say to me, "That one wasn't husband. Was
waste-band."'

Corinne bit her lip, smiled.

'The man disappear from my house and my bed for seven
days and seven nights.'

'A biblical man.'

'Biblical? I don't know. Was forty days and forty nights
Christ went for.'

'After this seven-day absence . . .' Corinne smiled in
anticipation. She had heard this story often.

'After this absence, I hear me door knock kow, kow, kow
one night. And, wait, stop laughing and listen, non. Wait.
This disappear you see he disappear there, we didn't have any
confusion, you know. He just decide to leave. I didn't even
bother to look for him; because I done hear already is so he is,
is things like that he would do. So I say, "Oh yes? Well, let's
see!" So this day when the door knock, I look outside. Friend,
is Mister, yes, standing on the step. I say to him,' and

Madelene lifted her chin, held up her right hand with an admonishing forefinger, ' "You go right back where you coming from. You know someone here? Go right back where you coming from!" '

Corinne giggled. 'What *really* happened after that, Auntie Madelene?'

'How you mean what *really* happened? Is like I always tell you. I say my piece and I leave him there.'

'So he just went away?'

'As far as I was concerned he could have stayed there if he wanted to. Wasn't my problem. Anyway, the last I heard of him he was in St Kitts by his people, I think.'

'Auntie Madelene, you never looked back? You never found out about him or anything?'

'Why? Is husband I want so? When people show they care nothing about you, what you looking back for?'

Madelene and Madge. Her aunt. Her mother. The weak and the gentle? The strong and the boisterous? Could I have done it? Corinne wondered. Just left him standing there? Perhaps if she hadn't really cared! Nonsense! As Auntie Madelene said, if a person show they don't care about you . . .

Madelene stood, stretched, switched on the gas fire. 'It's getting cold,' she said. 'You're staying over? Stay, non!'

Corinne thought for a moment. Why rush back to the apartment? In her mind, she surveyed the apartment. Had she put off the iron? Turned down the heat for when it came on? No lights on? She looked towards the window, where she could see nothing, really, but the curtains drawn. Against the cold. It would be cold outside. One of these days, she would get a car. Could get one fairly cheaply, and a good one, if she could find someone who knew their way around the garages.

'Okay. I'm on nights tomorrow. I can stay, yes. I'll leave in the morning. I'll stay.'

'Good. I'm glad for the company.' Madelene walked over to the window. Pulled aside the thick, red curtain, lifted the net and stood looking at the tall, grey buildings outside, up towards the distance where you couldn't even see a sky through the mist. She shivered.

A man walked by, light brown jacket, head uncovered, hands in pockets, head down. He was young. There was no way of telling what the weather was like from watching him. These young people wear the most ridiculous things in the cold. Two young women, thick, long coats, collar turned up, scarves, arms folded, heads down. It cold! Behind them, a middle-aged man, thick jacket, hood up, scarf, hands in pockets, shoulders hunched. It well cold!

'Look at me, eh!' Madelene said, turning back into the room. 'Look at me!' running her hand over the plastic tablecloth. '*Dimi millionaire na l'Amerik.*'

'Come again?'

Madelene chuckled, ran her hand along the waist of the thick trousers she usually wore during the cold evenings.

'When I used to take care of my grandmother, Grannie Belle, up on the hill in Hope, she was well disgusting. Your mother always say so, and was true, but poor thing. Nothing I do for her she ever used to be satisfied. That time my mother, your grandmother, was dead already. Grannie Belle used to say, "*Ich-mwen sé dimi millionaire na l'Amerik, zu ca ba mwen* 'inject' *shak jour!*" That time my father was up here, so what she saying to me was, "My son is a little millionaire in America; you here giving me 'inject' every day!" So now I say is me that is the little millionaire. Me self, yes, here in *l'Amerik.*'

'But what is "inject"?'

'The green banana they used to sell after they export what they consider good. They used to call the rest, what they selling to us, "reject", so she just didn't get the word good, and she called it "inject". Inject, reject, same thing.'

'My mother used to be with you at that time, Auntie Madelene?'

'At first. But she really didn't like it in that house. Your grandmother wasn't easy. She used to call us the worse names possible. And after she had the stroke and couldn't walk, she get even more miserable. She used to go down on the floor, sit down, and drag herself right across the floor. And sometimes if something annoy her, she would drag the centre table or anything she could pull or push, right across the floor. And if that back door open, she would push it right over. Right outside. It sounding funny now, but you know how often we run outside behind things and run down the hill over the sea there before things disappear?'

'Yes.'

Madelene sat down, her eyes staring at the wall opposite, but clearly not seeing it. 'I remember the tourists always used to stop and come up on the hill by us to take pictures. "Lovely spot," they used to say. "It must be a joy to you to live here; it's the most *divine* spot." '

Corinne said nothing. The old house was no longer there, she knew. But she had gone to Grenada with friends on two occasions, had taken them to that very spot over the sea. They had stayed at a guest house in St George's, the capital, although Corinne had stayed some nights by friends and distant relatives of her aunt. Had met people who kept saying things like, So this is Madge own, eh! Look at that, eh! These children and them doesn't take time to grow, non! And she look like the mother, eh! God ave is mercy! Child, you don't lose road at all!' Corinne smiled, remembering the voices, the faces, the unquestioning acceptance. On the occasions when they had gone to Hope, Corinne and her friends had walked down to the sea, back up again to sit in the sun and just gaze at the view. Corinne and her friends, too, had thought the view divine. If they had that, they said, they wouldn't live anywhere else.

It was when she thought about that sometimes that Corinne wondered if her aunt was serious about New York being her home. You couldn't come from a place like that and call New York home and really mean it! Could you? Even now, sometimes, Auntie Madelene would sit down looking dreamy and say, 'All those white people and them going out to the West Indies buying land and settling down in the sunshine! It nice in truth, yes.' And sometimes she would suck her teeth and say, 'Perhaps I better retire there in truth!' And laughingly she would ask Corinne, 'You will come too? Or visit me sometimes?' Sometimes Corinne didn't answer; sometimes she said, 'Of course I will come too!' And then her aunt just smiled and said, 'Of course? Of course?' And at times she added. 'I just joking, child! You have your own life!'

'After a while,' said Madelene now, 'your mother got a job working for a Mistress Anderson not so far away. Estate people, you know. So they used to live in the Great House. Grenada white. And that Mistress Anderson was a special lady.'

'Special how?' Corinne pulled Auntie Madelene's other pair of slippers from the corner by the television, slipped off her high-heeled shoes with a sigh.

'Specially mean,' explained Auntie Madelene, and Corinne laughed. 'She had two disgusting little boys that Madge was supposed to take care of. She was so mean that she didn't even want your mother and the other servants to use her pots to do their cooking. And she said she not boarding anyone; she paying them, so they not to eat her food. Find their own.'

'But she was sure taking a lot of chances! And she let them *cook* for her? Wasn't she afraid that they'd *do* something? Put something in the food or something? Come *on!*'

'Same thing Madge used to say. Come on is right! But some of these people were so important they didn't think they were dealing with people at all as long as you poor. And black wasn't nothing. So the servants would share the food for the family, and no chance to take something because she measuring everything she put out. She say she pay a few pence extra, so that they could find their own pots to do their own cooking. But *ki extra sa*? What extra is that?

'So your mother used to stay around and cook sometimes in one of the other servant's pot. But then I said to her, "Don't take her on; come down here and eat. Is an hour for lunch, so you will have time; don't stay up there. Come down!" Because what the lady used to do, you see, is that as she know Madge around, before the hour up, she going to sleep and she know the children will go to Madge and she will be looking after them. But that can't work. You can't let people take you and tie wood like that.

'So Madge started to come down to the village in Hope for lunch, and take her full lunch hour. And you don't know? The lady *then* offer her a little pot of her own, saying that she could stay up there and cook.'

'She didn't take it, of course?'

'Not at first. She tell me the lady could take the pot and put it back right under her bed or wherever she had it; but then the lady come and press her, press her, and I believe Madge self was afraid she lose the job, because job wasn't so easy to find that time, so eventually she come and take it.'

Corinne didn't say anything. She had never heard this story about her mother before. It didn't sound, somehow, like the big, tough mother she had come to believe existed in those early days. Fancy going back eventually and accepting the offer of that pot! Madelene looked at her niece's pensive face.

'You children don't know anything, you know,' she said, almost gently. 'You don't know trouble at all. Talking about things is one thing. Living it is another. When you have time to read about hardship and talk about it, always remember is because you don't have to live it.' Corinne looked at her aunt's face, at the lines running across her forehead, down at her hands. Madelene rubbed her hands together, pushed the fingers through each other. 'Because you don't have to live it,' she repeated softly.

She leaned back, cupped her hands at the base of her stomach again, and this time Corinne was very afraid. Her aunt looked so tired.

'Auntie Madelene,' Corinne said quickly, wanting to say something, anything. 'Tell me about my mother!'

Madelene kept her eyes closed. 'Your mother,' she said, 'sometimes I think I tell you as much as I could about her. She live a short life, she didn't even make it to forty. She barely pass thirty, in fact; she live a short time, but she live a lot. And she live strong, mostly, except when she close her eyes to life and forget.' Aunt Madelene opened her eyes and studied Corinne's face. 'You have her looks', she said, 'you have her looks, and you have a lot of her manner. She was strong, very strong like all of us. Like all of us, Corinne.' Aunt Madelene closed her eyes again. 'Except when she close her eyes and let somebody make her forget how much she go through already, and how much she could go through again. Except when she close her eyes and forget.'

'And Aunt Madelene,' said Corinne desperately, thinking that there were so many things she didn't know about her aunt and about that whole life back in Grenada, and feeling frightened because of the way Aunt Madelene was talking, 'tell me about you, now. Tell me some more about your life.'

'Tomorrow, child. We will always have a lot of time to talk. Tomorrow, if God spare life. And you young people don't have patience for all those old time stories, anyway. Tomorrow.'

'What do you mean we don't have patience?' Corinne was kneeling in front of her aunt's sofa, holding her hands in hers. 'I'm *asking* you, Auntie Madelene.'

Madelene opened her eyes briefly. Smiled gently at Corinne. 'Madge,' she said. Closed her eyes, and just when Corinne thought she was asleep, Aunt Madelene said, 'I know, honey. I know you care. I'm not as young and as strong as before. I'm a little bit tired, now. So tomorrow; okay? Everything have a pattern. We never miss nothing, really. Tomorrow, if God spare life.' Madelene placed her hand lightly on the younger woman's head, her thumb just touching Corinne's forehead.

The Walk

Faith reached up and unbuttoned the apron at the back. Let it drop to the front. Reached back and loosened the knot at her waist. Pulled off the apron and dropped it on to the barrel behind the door. She slumped on to the bench just inside of the kitchen door. She looked across at the fireside, at the scattered bits of wood, at the ashes cold and grey around the wood. Her eyes moved automatically towards the coal-pot, where a yellow butter-pan rested on partly burnt-out coals. She wondered whether Queen had prepared anything. To tell the truth, she was too tired to really care. She turned and looked at the bucket of water on the dresser, at the two pancups hanging from a nail above it. She took a deep breath, released it and let her head fall forward on to the rough board of the kitchen table.

'Oh God ah tired!' For a few moments, Faith remained like that, letting her body savour what it was like to be sitting down, letting it relax. And then her bottom registered that there was something hard on the bench. Faith's hand found the pebble, removed it. She sat up with a sigh and threw the pebble through the window over the shelf. Faith looked down at the floor. Yes. Queen had scrubbed it. A good child, when she put her mind to it.

Faith leaned back against the brown board of the partition and closed her eyes.

'Queen! Queenie oh! Bring some water give me!'

Queen came running. 'Mammie I didn't hear you come,

non! And I look out the back window and I see light in the Great House still, and I see a lot of cars go up, so I say they having party, and . . .'

'All right. All right!'

Faith held the pancup with both hands, drinking the water in great gulps.

'Ah! Dat good! You boil de cocoa tea?'

'Yes, Mammie.'

'The lady pay me dis evening. I want you to go up for me tomorrow mornin.'

Queen sucked her teeth. 'Mammie I . . .'

'You what?' Faith sat up, her eyes demanding the response they defied her daughter to make. 'Look, child! If you know what good for you, move out of me eyesight, eh! You have to go up for me tomorrow and pay de society, an Cousin Kamay have the little pig mindin so I could turn me hand to something. I want you to pass and see if it drop already. You remember de house where I did show you Cousin Sésé daughter livin?'

'De house wid de green gate and the yellow curtain in the window?'

'So if they change de curtain you won't know de house?'

'Ay! Yes, Mammie, it have a big mammie apple tree in the yard.'

'Right. Pass there and tell Cousin Sésé daughter, Miss Ivy, I ask if de message ready already.'

'Yes, Mammie.'

Faith looked at her daughter standing beside the bucket of water, at her bony, long-legged frame in the baggy dress. She sighed. It would be a long walk, but Queen was used to it. She wished she didn't have to take the child away from school to make these errands, but what with living so far away and not being able to get a job nearer to the family! And she *must* pay the society. If she dropped down tomorrow morning, what would happen to Queen? A person must make sure to put by a little. You never know when you time would come without warning! And if the pig drop now, she could sell one and have enough to at least buy a little bed. And perhaps she might even be able to take out a better susu hand. Anyway, don't count you chickens! Just hope for the best. Just hope!

'Don't drink too much water, Queen. Next thing you know, you playin baby give me an wetting you bed. Is time for you to go an sleep. You have to get up early. You drink the coraile bush for the cold?'

'Yes, Mammie, an I make some bakes and put in de safe.'

'Good. That good. You a real help to me, yes. I don't know what I would do without you, child! Take de small lamp an go inside and sleep. Leave de masanto here for me. What light you sit down inside there with? You have a candle?'

'No, Mammie, I was just sitting down looking out of the back window at the Great House lights.'

'Sitting down in the dark, Queen? Why you didn't take the small lamp all the time?'

'Was only for a little while, yes, Mammie, after I finish clean up the kitchen.'

'All right, go on! Go on and get ready for bed!'

Queen took the lamp and walked out of the kitchen door. For just a moment she glanced to the left, at the quiet, dark outline of coconut trees. But she didn't like the way the coconut trees rustled, and besides you could never trust a sudden breeze not to put the lamplight out.

Queen climbed the two wooden steps into the house, placed the lamp on the shelf and prepared for bed. She was thinking of the following morning's walk as she pulled the pile of bedding from under the sofa in the corner and spread it out. Queen did not like having to walk all the way to River Sallee. The road was long. She was always afraid to walk that long road. Queen stood for a long while staring at the lamp. She looked at the partition above the lamp, at the picture which had written on it, *God Save Our Gracious King*. Thrown over the top of this picture was her mother's chaplet, the cross resting on the king's forehead. Queen wasn't really *seeing* the picture. She was thinking. Wondering who and who was going to make that walk to River Sallee with her tomorrow morning. Who else was going up? In her hand was the old, torn dress that her mother no longer wore and which she was about to spread out on the floor over the other things already there. Queen walked to the door, her dress band trailing. She had already undone the fastener at the back, and the dress was drooping, baring one bony shoulder.

'Mammie! Cousin Liza goin up tomorrow too?'

'Yes. She goin to call for you early in the morning. You say you prayers yet?'

'No Mammie. I goin an say it now.'

Queen changed quickly, knelt down, bent her forehead to touch the sofa, and prayed aloud: 'Gentle Jesus meek and mild, look upon a little child!'

She lifted her head and looked at the crucifix over the bed. 'Papa God, help me to grow up into a big strong girl for me please. God don't let me die tonight or any other night please. Bless Mammie and Cousin Dinah and Maisie and Mark. Make the walk tomorrow not hard please and don't let me and Cousin Liza meet anything in the road. Bless Cousin Liza too and let me have a lot a lot of money when I get big please God. Amen.'

Still on her knees, Queen lifted her head.

'Good-night, Mammie.'

'Good-night, chile. Turn down de lamp low.'

'You not goin an sleep now, Mammie?'

'Yes. I just takin a little rest fus.'

'Well come and rest inside here, non, Mammie.'

'Queenie hush you mouth an sleep now. You pray already. Stop talkin like dat after you pray.'

About an hour later, Faith, having eaten some of the bake from the safe and allowed the day's weariness to seep from her body through the boards to the still, hot air outside, walked heavily up the two board steps and into the house. There was some noise as she passed briefly through the watching darkness; a cat scuttling, perhaps, a dog scratching, a frog hopping by. Faith didn't look around. She hardly heard them. The sounds of darkness were always with her. Nothing strange.

Her young Queen was fast asleep, mouth slightly open, left hand thrown wide and resting on the floor outside the bedding, the cover partly twisted around her waist. The mother stood staring for a moment, then stooped to straighten the piece of bedding which served as a cover and pulled it up over her daughter's body. She turned to the sofa, then sank to her knees and bowed her head. Faith spoke no words aloud. She talked silently to the Lord. Her last waking thoughts were, Today is the madam party. I wonder if Mr Mark suit . . .

When Cousin Liza pounded at the door on that February morning in 1931, it was still the time of day when everyone whispered. Dark and cold in the kind of way it never was when the sun came up. It was still the time that the trees claimed as their own as they whispered secrets against the sky. They whispered something when Cousin Liza knocked, and she looked around nervously, but they became silent then.

The walk from St David's to River Sallee was a long and arduous one. It was best started early. Queen was still half-asleep when they left. But the way Cousin Liza walked, sleep didn't stay around for long. It departed with a frown and an irritated yawn. Wide awake after the first few mintues, Queen pushed the straw hat more firmly on to her head, held the cloth bag securely on her shoulder, and kept running to keep up.

Cousin Liza had planned to start at five am. She must have made a mistake, though. Day was a long time coming, and the trees and the shadows and the frogs shouting in the drains kept insisting that it was still their time. They had been walking for more than two hours when the first glimmers of dawn appeared. At one time they had passed a house in which a light burned brightly. The man inside may have seen them, for the door was open. Into the darkness he shouted, 'Wey dis two woman goin at this hour?' and his feet pounded on the floor as though he were coming out to get them. If she had known who he was, Cousin Liza wouldn't be afraid, but you never knew with people who were up that late. They could be doing all sorts of things with the supernatural. So Cousin Liza pulled Queen and they pelted off down the road, feet flying on the broken pavement. After this, Queen was afraid, for she realised that Cousin Liza, too, walked with fear.

At one point, when they got to a place where the road forked in three directions, Queen did not find it strange to see a cock standing in the middle of the crossroads. She was accustomed to fowls. It was only when she felt Cousin Liza jerk her towards the drain that she froze. They passed in the drain at the side of the road and walked without looking back. Cousin Liza did not have to tell Queen it would be dangerous to look back. She *knew*! Queen's whole body was heart. It pounded with a painful thump that resounded in her steps. Her bare feet felt neither the stones in the road nor the effect of the miles. Suspended in a twilight between conscious thought and puppetry, she knew neither where she was nor where she was going to. And worse was yet to come.

They were making their way through a track in Hope, St Andrew's, which could cut down on the distance to Grenville town, when Queen pulled convulsively on Cousin Liza's hand. Liza's twenty-eight years on what she knew of earth had not given her the fearlessness that Queen expected her to possess. Queen stood, one hand now on top of the straw hat the brim of which framed her round face, the thick black plaits sticking out on both sides, the other hand lifted towards the distance. Liza froze. With a taut, tense movement she boxed down the child's shaking finger.

'Don't point,' she whispered hoarsely. 'Bite you finger,' she remembered to add.

On the hill next to the gravestone, something moved. No house was in sight. Above the watching women, the branches of the trees leaned across and linked leaves, touching each other caressingly in the stillness of the morning. The thing moved again. A pale light from a wandering, waning moon flashed across it and the thing bent towards them, beckoning, encouraging them forward. Queen's arms were thrown around Liza and she clung tightly, mouth open, the breath pushed from her throat to her lips in audible sobs, eyes wide with terror. Liza, body and hands hard with fear, held on to the child. She uttered no prayer with her lips, none in her heart. Her whole body was a throbbing prayer. Papa God! Papa God!

Whatever it was was quiet now. Still, no longer beckoning. The leaves above, too, had stopped their furtive caressing. Liza's feet moved. One quiet dragging step. Two, the left foot following because it couldn't go off on its own in a different direction. T-h-r-ee. Queen's body, with no will or separate identity of its own, did whatever Liza's did. The thing bent towards them. Queen screamed. With sudden decision, Liza dragged Queen along the edge of the track. And as this living fear drew level with the taunting thing above, it stopped in unbelief.

'Jesus!' said Cousin Liza. 'Jesus!'

The plantain leaf bowed again.

Queen, sobbing now with the release of terror, clung to Cousin Liza's hand and was dragged along the track. Her destination was daylight. It was only when the sky lightened and she could hear cocks crowing and see people moving about in the yards that she became once more a conscious being. She started to feel tired and told Cousin Liza that she wanted to rest.

They had been walking for seven hours and were in Paradise with the sun blazing down upon their heads when the bus from St David's passed them on its way to Sauteurs. Queen ate her coconut-drops and stretched out her tongue at the people looking back from the back seat of the bus. Years later, an older Queen learnt that the threepence she and Cousin Liza had spent to buy things to eat along the way could have paid a bus fare. Even though she had known then, the knowledge would have been of little use. Faith would have called her damn lazy if she had suggested going by bus.

'Liza, girl, you must be tired. How you do? Come, come, come girl. Come an sit down. Queenie, child, me mind did tell me you mother would send you up today.'

Cousin Kamay accepted their arrival as a matter of course.

'Constance, put some food in the bowl for Cousin Liza. Go in the kitchen an see what you get to eat, Queen. It have food dey. Help youself to what you want. How you mother?'

'She well tanks.'

'Well tanks *who*?'

'She well tanks, Cousin Kamay.'

Cousin Kamay watched her. 'Hm! You gettin big! These children nowadays you have to keep a eye on them yes. Go an see what you get to eat!'

The journey was over. In two days' time, after being about her mother's business, eleven-year-old Queen would leave again with Cousin Liza or whoever else happened to be making the trip to St David's. The one thing that remained to haunt her was the knowledge that the return trip would have to be made in darkness, when the sun was down, and when those who had to walk always made their journeys.

Gemini

Nadie was ten years old when first she became aware of Gemini's existence. In fact, it was the twenty-ninth of May, the day of her tenth birthday.

She had dreamt of a hill the night before. Had stood at the bottom of the hill and looked up. Up and up towards the top almost hidden by the clouds. Or was it the sky? Up there was something bluish. Mist? It *may* have been the clouds. Nadie had tried to climb the hill. Had walked and walked and walked and when she looked around had realised that she hadn't moved. Had closed her eyes and walked faster. Opened them and found that she still hadn't moved. And the hill must have become River Hill, up which she walked every morning on her way to school, only that it was higher than River Hill, but when she looked to the left there was the same bridge with the boys talking and laughing, some sitting watching her, others standing with their arms folded leaning back against the big stone on the corner. Just like they did every afternoon. *She hadn't moved.*

That was when she had screamed. Or had tried to scream. Because although she knew she was afraid and wanted badly to scream, she couldn't. She had tried and tried and tried and struggled against not screaming. And then she had been half awake, aware that she was still trying to scream, but something was holding her to the bed; her feet and hands were tied; she was being strangled and her voice couldn't, couldn't . . . With an effort bigger than her ten years, Nadie pushed away the restraining force and sat up, wide-eyed, shivering and afraid.

Her first waking thought was, Today is my birthday! She stood, walked two steps towards the door, and looked back over her shoulder towards the bed. Her mouth was slightly opened, the gap between her front teeth clearly visible; her black eyes were liquid and weak with fear. People said that when that happened, when you tried to get up and felt as if someone was holding you down on the bed, it was because you were being attacked by a loupgarou. Loupgarou was tying you down to suck away your blood. Suppose – suppose – Nadie turned abruptly away from the bed, towards the door. She screamed. Someone was standing there. Nadie put her hand over her mouth, backed towards the bed, sat down and burst into tears.

'What's wrong with you?' her mother asked, moving towards the window and lifting the net curtains on to the nail at the side, so that even more light came into the room. 'What happen? I hear you moving about. It's only half past five, although it so bright outside already. How you get up so early? What happen? What happen to you?'

'I didn't know was you,' whispered Nadie.

'So that's why you crying? What happen?'

'I couldn't sleep.'

'You had a bad dream?'

'Yes. Yes, Mai,' Nadie sniffed, 'I had a bad dream.'

'Don't wipe you nose on you nightie, Nadie. Come on, you know better than that. There's some toilet paper on the table there. Use that.' Mai stood looking through the window-panes for a moment, lifted the nets off the nail and let them fall gently across the window.

Nadie sniffed and blew her nose.

'You had a nightmare?'

'Yes,' Nadie sobbed. 'Yes, Mai. I had a nightmare. A bad, bad, bad nightmare.'

Mai didn't seem to get more sympathetic because the nightmare had been three or four times as bad as might be expected. 'Is all this green mango you been eating last night. I tell you it would upset your stomach. Go on, lie down. Lie down. You could stay in bed for a while still. Get up by half past six and be in plenty of time for school. Lie down, let me pull the sheet over you.'

'I don't want to sleep again, Mai. It was as if – as if – loupgarou was tying me down to the bed.'

'Nonsense. Loupgarou what? You taking all nonsense you hear making it frighten you. Is the green mango riding you stomach that is the loupgarou. Go back to sleep. I will sit down here on the bed for a while. Go to sleep. I will wake you up in time for school.'

It rained that day. Started raining at six o'clock, just before Nadie fell asleep and, according to Mai, fell 'bucket a drop' the whole time.

The old house in the yard opposite was drenched to a muddy-brown. It looked like it would just collapse with weeping if you tried to wring the rainwater from its boards. The breadfruit tree behind it was weeping, too, its bright green leaves full of glistening rain-tears which rolled off every so often on to the rusty galvanize; the banana leaves swung gently, drops glinting and racing across their green faces. The rain fell from the rooftops on to the grass around Mai's house, making little pools of water here and there where the grass was driest. The water filled the drains for miles around and raced across the roads.

Everywhere, on that birthday morning, people turned over in their beds, looked up at their windows, breathed deeply, and pulled the sheets over their heads. The sight and sound of rain made a person feel colder. No work today. No school today.

It was eight o'clock when Mai woke Nadie up. Eight o'clock and Nadie yawned as she watched the rain hitting against her window-pane. She thought of the rhyme in her school book,

Rain, rain, go away,
Come again another day.

No. no. Her mind danced away. Don't think of that. Who
wants the rain to stop?

Fly away Peter
Fly away Paul

Nadie frowned. Why had she thought of that? What did Peter
and Paul have to do with it? There was a game like that.
Perhaps St Peter and St Paul could make sure that the rain
didn't stop.

A holiday! Tang, tang! A flipping holiday . . . As always,
when her mind dashed away and said its own things like that,
Nadie glanced at the doorway quickly, at least in the direction
of where she knew her mother to be, and said quickly to
herself, Not me, non, Mai, is me mind. I don't know what
does do it at all! Then she got up and danced around her
room. Tang, tang! A holiday on me blasted birthday! Her
mind was going too far now. Jeezan Bread! what kind of
mind is this? Child you mind tear up? All how I try to make
you into somebody you going you own sweet good-for-
nothing way! Nadie collapsed on to her bed, giggling.

'Nadie?'

'Mai?'

'You and who inside there?'

'Aw! What do Mai? Me and who that could be there?'

'Don't bring you rudeness give me. That is what *I* wondering. Is only mad people and old people with memories that
does talk to theyself like that, and you're neither, so stop you
nonsense.'

Nadie giggled. 'Aw!' she said, in a voice so tiny that even
the moth caught by daylight still fluttering on the little shelf
near to the small lamp whose light had gone out since last
night couldn't hear her. 'Aw! What do Mai at all? She drink
Jeyes or something? So I don't have me memories too, then?'

'Ma*dam*! You smelling youself this morning?'

Nadie couldn't believe it! Mai *couldn't* hear that!

'What happen, Mai? What I do?' Nadie had to find out. She looked towards the door, listening, waiting. 'I don't do nothing, non! What happen, Mai?'

'Don't form the fool with me, eh, child! Get outa you bed come out here and wash up yourself!'

Nadie didn't giggle this time. She only smiled. And spoke to herself. Not in any secret, but inside this time. You this Mai? People mustn't take chances with you, non. Where you see you siddown playing you reading Bible dey, you ears open for every little grunt people belly make! This time she chuckled. And waited. Daring Mai to say something to *that*! But Mai didn't say anything.

Nadie stretched. A holiday! A holiday on her birthday! Well I ain't playin lucky, non! Some people just born with a gold spoon! In their mouth, in their nose, any flipping place. Nadie laughed again. With satisfaction. 'Flipping' came out at will any old time now, and it felt good, having this place inside of you to shout flipping without Mai even guessing! God's in his heaven; all's right with the world. She had heard or read that somewhere. The thought sobered her. She felt like stretching again and didn't even stretch. People didn't fool around with God. Fancy a person just knowing every-thing you do! Like if you raise up you dress in secret and scratch you belly! Or dig you finger in you nose and eat it! Or stoop down on the side of the road and pull down you pantie and pee in the grass when you really want to go to the toilet and can't wait! Jeezan ages! Fancy God just staying there and watching that! Nadie wasn't very sure what God would think about her thoughts now, especially as she could feel her mind coming up with a description of God that she just couldn't let it say when you thought about people turning into pillars of salt and things like that. So she closed her eyes hard and bit her lips against the irreverent thought, made the sign of the cross quickly, and said 'I don't mean nothing, non. I don't mean nothing in truth. I just thinking.'

That was the one major frightening difference between Mai and God. Mai could hear even when you whispered. God could flip. . . Nadie cleared her throat and started the thought again, trying not to wonder if God had been fooled. God could hear even when you *didn't* whisper. That is one hell of a. . . Nadie frowned. Really! Standing on the side of God, Nadie glared warningly at her irreverent mind. That, she started again, and finished safely this time, is one person!

Nadie sighed, pulled up the covers, turned over on to her side, pulled her knees up under her chin, and let the rain soothe her almost back to sleep.

'Nadie? Get up, my dear. Don't sleep for the whole day. Happy Birthday, child! Happy, Happy Birthday!'

Nadie jumped out of bed.

'Oh yes! You know I did nearly forget? I remember this morning early and then I forget! Oh yes! Is me birthday! I have ten years today.'

'Ten full years, Madam. You are a big lady now.'

'Tang, tang,' Nadie sang, 'birth-day.' One thing with Mai, whatever she say to you the rest of the year, however she might rag up a person, your birthday was yours! That was the gift, and to Nadie, it was the greatest gift. You would have to really try to get rag up for something on your birthday. Of course, nowadays Mai liked to talk to a person a lot. Nadie dropped her nightie on to the floor and sat down slowly, naked, on the bed. She watched the drops on the window. She watched a bird hover and kiss a bright yellow flower turning its face to the sun outside. Mai liked to talk these days about *boys* and things, and for sure she would talk today.

'You reach the age of reason now,' Mai was saying, from out in the living room beyond the closed door of Nadie's bedroom. 'More than reason. No more nonsense. You not no little child no more. You're becoming a big lady now.'

Nadie frowned, picked up her nightie and flung it at the door.

'Yes, my child,' said Mai quietly, 'the age of reason.'

Nadie put up both hands and pulled back the sides of her

mouth as she glared at the door. She heard God saying something like, 'You don't do things like that when your mother speak to you.' And Nadie heard herself saying 'Ah, chuts,' right after Mai said, 'You must be careful with boys!'

Mai said, 'What!' Nadie wasn't sure whether she had said it to Mai or to God, but it couldn't have been either, so it *must* have been this other thing, so she wasn't telling a lie at all, really, when she said, 'Mai, is not you, non. Is as I putting on the dress and is as if a button fall out or something, yes,' and just at that moment Nadie pulled hard enough and a button did really fall out, so it *wasn't* a lie, really.

'It better not be me you talking to, in truth,' and this time the door was opened and Mai was standing there with her Bible in her hand. And sure enough God was with her. And the cross over the door just over Mai's head made it feel to Nadie like judgment day. And the worst thing was, Mai was wearing a mauve dressing-gown just like the priest's vestment sometimes.

Nadie opened her hand with the button lying on her palm and said to Mai and God, 'Watch! Just so the button fall out!'

Mai looked at her funny like, as if she wasn't too interested in the button, and didn't much like Nadie's explanation. Then she and her Bible went back out through the door. Nadie sighed. Thank God is me birthday. Papa God, you know me. I ain't pretending nothing, but you know I don't mean nothing. Thanks, yes.

She couldn't go out into the living room just yet. The day was starting funny. Maybe because she was ten. Nadie propped the pillows up against the back of the bed, sat down, drew up her legs, hugged them with her hands, and through the net curtains watched the rain hitting angrily against both windows. Only some drops managed to actually make it to hit the window panes. The eaves over the windows kept most of them away, but the rain was so heavy and the wind so high that some of the huge drops hit the window suddenly, like a – like a cuff from her mother's hand when she was angry – and then dissolved and ran crying down the window-pane.

Nadie was glad to see the rain, even though it also made her feel sort of quiet and sad when she stopped to watch it, like now. She was glad even if it meant there would be no lessons and nobody to play with. 'It not healthy to have one child,' her Uncle Dan had once said to her mother when he visited them. Short, stocky Uncle Dan with his high forehead and laughing eyes. The only man who she could say was her mother's real friend. He ignored her when she quarrelled with him and kept visiting. Sometimes they wouldn't see him for a long time, but then he turned up with a shout. 'Mai! What going on, girl?' And even though Mai would shout, 'You nastiness! Where you turn up from like Christmas all of a sudden to confuse people? Go you way!' You could tell she was glad to see him. And Uncle Dan would just laugh, and usually he would fling one leg over the banister and sit there like that halfway on the verandah, talking to them until he felt like leaving.

'Time for you to have another one,' he had said. 'Not on your life,' her mother had answered. 'For another dirtiness like you worthless brother? Not on your life.' Was her uncle a 'dirtiness' too? Or was it just his brother, her father, to whom Mai never talked?

Once, when Nadie was about seven, she had come home talking about Daddy. She had met him in the street; he was drunk; he had told his friends, 'There goes my daughter. There goes my fine, upstanding scholar of a daughter, even if she and she mother too proud to know me! Young as she is, dey, she could read good, you hear!' And he had walked towards Nadie and said, 'Child, remember me. Honour thy father!' pointing a warning finger at her. And then he had put his hand into his pocket, saying, 'Here, here!' Had pulled it out and given her twenty-five cents. Nadie giggled quietly. When she got home that day, talking about Daddy and showing her mother the twenty-five cents, Mai was like, like, a cat on a hot tin roof. Like a cat on a hot tin roof! That is what Mai always said when a person was *really* vex. She would say, 'She couldn't stay quiet, she was so vex; she just keep turning round like a cat on a hot tin roof!' And that is how Mai was that day. Boy, she was vex!

'Tell you brother,' Mai had said later to Uncle Dan, 'tell you brother! If he want to know who I *really* is, start to interfere between me and me child! Where he suddenly come out playing father?' And Uncle Dan had only laughed, singing, 'Never, never put you mouth . . .' Mai hadn't laughed. She was really vexed.

But that other time when her uncle had visited, it was around Christmas and they were cleaning sorrel. Mai had pulled off the prickly green bits from around the blood-red sorrel petals, stripped the bud open, pulled out and dumped the seed into the waste basket, and looked angry as she dropped the petals into the bowl. 'Not on your bleeding life,' her mother had said. Imagine! 'Not on your *bleeding* life!' Mai didn't usually say things like bleeding when she knew that Nadie could hear her. Although Nadie had heard her say worse than that when she thought she wasn't around.

Nadie rolled over, stifling her chuckles in the pillow. Like the time when she had come home from school and Mai hadn't seen her standing behind the mango tree. Nadie had heard her shouting to Trevor from down in the land by Miss Miriam. *Trevor*, you know! Big, bad Trevor who everybody fraid and who they say does thief all people thing and they can't tell him nothing. 'You plant any flipping fig tree here so that you could come and cut banana when you ass-hole please? Look, eh, man, just leave me kiss-me-arse fig where you see it until I ready to eat it, eh! And another thing, so help me God, Trevor, if I miss one more fowl from outa me yard, people go just hear you crowing in the street every time you pass me house. You hear me?' Trevor, you know! Trevor, Mai speak to like that. Nadie giggled. Trevor must be did well thief the fowl and banana in truth because he didn't say not a word; he just move off like a cut-tail dog as if he fraid people see him and as if, Nadie chuckled, as if he fraid fowl crow inside he belly in truth.

Nadie turned over and lay looking at the ceiling, at the

spots where the moths had hit and left their mark. That day,
last Christmas, Nadie was sitting right there at the table with
Mai, helping her clean the sorrel, and she had said 'bleeding'
just like that. It hadn't been easy to drink the sorrel after that.
It had tasted of blood. It was as if she had given her hand one
big cut and was sucking up all of the blood. She had only
tasted a little sorrel that Christmas, and only because she
couldn't bear it if Christmas passed and she didn't taste
everything that Mai made. But she had drunk mainly ginger
beer, adding water so that it didn't taste so strong.

It not healthy to have one child. Nadie wondered why. She
didn't think she missed other children. In fact, she was sure
she didn't miss them. Today, for example, what she would
really miss were her lessons – the dictation and the reading and
the arithmetic – not the playground and the children in the
class.

In school it was different. She didn't even stretch out her
tongue in secret to the teachers like she did at Mai at home.
School frightened her. Not the lessons, but the people. The
people. Nadie's elbows were on the pillow, her palms turned
towards her face; she rubbed at her eyebrows with her wrists,
lifted her legs one after the other and hit gently against the
bed. She was almost afraid of the children. A little bit afraid of
those in her class and a whole lot afraid of those in other
classes.

Once – last year, in fact, when she was in Standard V –
Miss had really praised Nadie in class one day. She had said
that Nadie's arithmetic was not just good, it was outstanding.
Nadie had kept her head down, feeling stupid. She had felt
really bad when Miss had held up Karen's exercise book with
a lot of red crosses across the page. Miss had held it up so that
the class could see. 'This,' Miss had said, 'is the exact opposite
of Nadie's. This,' and Miss had pinched Karen's exercise
book between her thumb and forefinger, holding it just at the
top of its spine as if she didn't really want to touch it, 'is a
perfect example of how *not* to do arithmetic.' And Miss had
given Karen, who sat next to Nadie, three hot ones in the

palm of her hand with the thick ruler.

Nadie had felt miserable for the rest of that arithmetic class. Not just felt miserable outside and big and bad inside like sometimes when Mai beat her, but really miserable inside and out. And Karen had looked at her cross-eyed and moved her chair and desk ever so slightly away.

Afterwards, when they were in the playground, Nadie had agreed with the others that Miss was a real 'curry favour' teacher. There were some children she liked, and she always gave them their sums right, and there were some children she didn't like and they could never do anything right. Then Nadie had realised that they were standing right under their classroom window. She looked up and she could see the back of Miss's head. Miss was standing right there, leaning back against the partition. Oh Lordy! Nadie said to herself. And is not even true!

Mai had gone through all of the sums with her at home; they had worked them together over and over until Nadie understood them; they had even done the proving together to make sure. So Nadie knew that her sums were really right. But still, when somebody said again, 'Boy, Miss is something else, yes,' Nadie only said, 'I tell you! True, yes, true.' And she felt worse than Trevor looked that day when Mai cursed him off.

That had happened the October. Nadie was glad then that December was so near, and that after December she would be leaving the school and going to high school.

She liked the lessons at school; Mai always helped her and made her do a lot of work at home and it wasn't hard. She just didn't like the people – the children and the teachers and the headmistress and so. Not that she didn't *like* them, really. It was just that they made her feel stupid and she had to pretend a lot and she always felt as if people wouldn't like her if they really knew her. And she was so frightened that she didn't even talk to them rude and jokey sometimes like she did with Mai, and in secret to herself sometimes. No. She just didn't like school. Not school. But people! Nadie rubbed at her eyes. People!

Some children were nice, though. Like Bianca sometimes. Bianca's mother was Miss Vie, Mai's friend. And sometimes she and Bianca would sit on the verandah talking while Miss Vie and Mai talked and laughed inside. She and Bianca talked about all kinds of things, even about babies. Nadie looked quickly at the door. If Mai knew! She and Bianca played catch sometimes; in the playground or even on the way home from school; sometimes they played hopscotch in the middle of the road! Nadie smiled, thinking of how car drivers shouted when they had to hoot loudly on their horns to get them out of the road. But then sometimes when they played rounders with all the other children even Bianca would call her things like 'slow-coach' and when she failed to catch the ball would say, 'Woy, that is a sieve?' Even Bianca! Nadie teased the other children sometimes. But not Bianca. Never! Nadie frowned, put her forehead down on her hands. Never!

'So Nadie, what happen? Because it's your birthday you not getting up this morning?'

'Yes, Mai. I up already, yes.'

'Well come on out! Brush your teeth, and take a wash and things like that. So is younger you're getting, then? I have to tell you what to do?'

'No, Mai. Coming now!'

As Nadie expected, that morning's breakfast was scrumptious. There was papaya from the tree outside, and a big fish fried with onions and tomatoes, and then there was some little titiri fried up like fish-cakes and bread which Mai had baked the day before. Birthdays were really the best! You could eat and drink exactly what you liked. Even as fast as you liked. Nadie ate fast, swallowing as loudly as she could and biting again; no response from Mai. She ate slowly, humming as she did so, and watching Mai from underneath her brows; no response. She held the bread and tore it with a grunt and then gobbled it up as the dog did outside sometimes. She was tempted to let the saliva drip down the sides of her mouth, too, but felt that might be going too far. Mai just appeared not to see. Nadie sighed. Oh, birthdays! She even asked for orange juice instead of cocoa tea and not a note from Mai. She got the juice.

After breakfast, or at least almost after breakfast, just as Nadie was reaching across for the last, juicy-looking fry titiri on the plate, Mai asked, 'You had a good breakfast, Nadie?'

The Nadie that Mai couldn't hear answered, 'Well fancy that! You see me gobbling up the last piece of titiri here and wondering if I better go down by the river and help them fish for more and you go ask me a question like that!'

The other Nadie, the one that usually spoke to Mai, said, 'Bestest, Mai. *Bestest*.'

'It obviously didn't do nothing for your English language. That gone out of the window. Don't play with me, child,' as Nadie eased up from her chair to peep outside of the window in search of her English. Nadie giggled.

'You are my one treasure. I want you to remember that.'

'Oh Lordy!' the other Nadie exclaimed. 'I think I getting out of here, yes.'

'You want me to help you wash the dishes, Mai?' Mai's Nadie asked in a small voice.

'No. It's your birthday. Is all right. In this weather I won't go to work today. I will wash them. Sit down. I want to have a little talk with you.'

'Oh, France!' said one Nadie, while the one sitting with Mai sighed and sank lower into her chair.

Nadie glanced at her mother's face. Looked away again. Through the window opposite where she sat was the broken-down old house that Mai said used to belong to her grand-parents. The rain, the wind, the sun had darkened the boards over time to a deep earth-brown. And the rain this morning made it look soggy. Old board, her mother always said, solid, solid. From the mountain. Not like the paper they making today. It last forever if you give it a chance. The galvanize covering the house was rusty. Now the water was dripping over the sides, making the house look really sad and weepy. Watching it, Nadie stretched her bottom lip far out, and frowned, lowering her brows, trying to make her face look like what the house looked like. Grandpa, who Mai said had lived eleven months longer than Grandma, had died six years ago. Nadie couldn't remember him. She couldn't remember either of them. Mai said that it was only stubbornness that had kept them living in that house, because it was then already leaky and shaking on the posts which held it off the ground.

Mai had just left it alone; she had cleared out the few belongings which her grandparents had acquired in seventy or so years of their existence, forty-one of them together, locked the door and left it locked. Not that the lock made a difference. Two boards were missing from the side of the house. Once, the dogs used to jump through them and shelter when the rains came. They no longer did this. The rains came through anyway and the two-roomed house looked about to fall.

Mai had said something else, too, that Nadie remembered. She had said in a kind of sad way that those two were like two peas in a pod. They quarrelled sometimes, but nothing could separate them. 'Was a ole-time love,' Mai said. 'You don't find that kind of thing these days.' Since after Mai said that, anytime Nadie shelled peas, she made sure that two of the peas from at least one pod were put down carefully in the bowl, so that they stayed together. And sometimes she stood by the peas tree just in front of the old house and imagined she could hear the peas in the pod quarrelling. She would frown and turn right around, saying 'Now, now, behave yourself. You know you love each other, so behave yourselves.'

People said that Grandma and Grandpa – Great Grandma and Great Grandpa – still lived in the house, and that sometimes at night they could be heard whispering together about how their only granddaughter had let them down, and taken example off the street and become baby mother at eighteen. Their one grandchild! The sins of the parents! The sins of the parents! Who could escape the punishment of the Lord? That's what people said the ghosts whispered. One day

Nadie had even heard a lady telling Miss Vie that in the market, when she and Bianca had gone out with Miss Vie. Miss Vie hadn't said anything, though. Just said to the lady in her slow way, 'Well all right, eh, I must try and get these few things and get back home. We will see.' And then she had glanced across at Nadie standing there looking at the tray of breadnuts. Nadie could see her out of the corner of her eyes and she knew that Miss Vie was wondering if she had heard. Nadie had asked her mother what the people meant. Mai said only, 'I never knew my mother. She died when I was born. I don't know who my father is.' Nadie wasn't sure if this was an answer to her question, or if her mother had just not answered. But she sensed that this had something to do with the sins of the parents!

Nadie crossed and uncrossed her legs under the chair, lowered her head, pressed her hands down on the chair on either side just under her bottom, pulled her shoulders up to her ears, lowered her shoulders. She moved her hands off the chair along her legs and glanced quickly again at her mother's face.

Mai's eyes were so sad! 'Jeezan ages!' said that mind of hers. 'What going on now?' And then Nadie wanted to cry. Mai sat looking far, far away. Nadie frowned. And while she sat struggling against the tears, her mind shouted impatiently, 'Start, non, Mai; start so you could finish quick.'

'Child,' Mai said. 'You ten today.'

'Whole day,' said the other Nadie. 'Whole flipping day.'

'You growing up,' said Mai. 'Life not easy. There are a lot of things out there just waiting to grab hold of you.'

Loupgarou, la diablesse an ting!

Nadie frowned.

'The older you get, the more you have to remember that life not easy.'

Nadie began to pout. It was at times like this that Mai called her rude. When Mai started these talks, Nadie couldn't listen without pouting, or sucking her teeth. Or sometimes the other Nadie took hold of her and made her throw a knife or fork or something on to the floor. Once, she just took up a plate and dashed it against the kitchen floor. Mai had whipped her that day and made her clear away the splinters. Nadie had wept. But had ended up swallowing her sobs and playing at laugh-cry with the unseen Nadie.

Now Mai was looking into the distance over by the door as if she was staring at someting there and didn't remember Nadie. Nadie hunched her shoulders, put her head down, and surreptitiously looked around towards the doorway.

'Child!' Mai started again, 'child, I was just like you once. Looking just like you and innocent just so! And is not so long ago, non. Is not long at all.'

'About twelve hundred million years?' the other Nadie speculated.

Mai leaned over and smoothed Nadie's eyebrows with her fingers. Both Nadies flinched and hunched their shoulders.

'Life does go fast, Nadie. But you take it slow, you hear. You don't have to run. I looking out for you. Look out for yourself, too. All right?'

'Yes, Mai.'

'You know,' Mai hesitated, as if she wasn't sure what else to say.

Oh God, Mai, make haste, non!

'Yes, Mai?'

'You must start taking more pride in yourself than you taking at present. Don't wait for me to tell you to do everything. I want you to grow up to be somebody important, Nadie. Somebody really important. Okay?'

'Yes, Mai.'

Nadie suppressed a giggle. And honestly, she didn't know why.

'So is joke I joking with you then? Is a joke to you to think of becoming somebody important?

'No, Mai, is not that, non.'

'It better not be that. Because you will make something of yourself if I have to drag you by the nose to do it!'

Nadie tried not to giggle again.

'Yes, Mai.'

'You must want good for yourself too and behave in such a way that you will get it.' Mai smoothed the plastic tablecloth with her left hand, put her left elbow on the table and cupped her chin in the palm of her hand. 'Such a way that you will get it, Nadie,' she repeated. Mai leaned forward, looking more closely at Nadie's face. She put her hand down, stretched out her right hand to Nadie's face. Nadie flinched, moving away. She didn't like it when Mai touched her. And this always made her feel guilty.

'Stay still. Stay quiet, child.' Mai wiped at the corner of Nadie's left eye with her finger. 'Look at you! Ten full years old and you not even washing you face properly! Look at all of this yampi in the corner of you eye! That is any way for little girl to come to table? You must take a pride in youself, Nadie.'

Nadie scowled.

'Take a pride in youself,' said Mai again, leaning back in her chair. 'Meself sometimes I don't know, non! I want so much for you, but you have to want it for yourself, too. You old enough now.' Mai propped her chin in her right hand this time and looked through the window at the old house. 'Yes,' she continued, 'you old enough now. Start to take a pride in youself, child. You are my one treasure. My one treasure.'

'So me is a treasure chest now!' This time the other Nadie talked so loudly that Mai's Nadie glanced quickly at her mother's face. No sign. Nadie bent forward, looked down towards the floor beside her chair, pulled up her shoulders and rubbed at her ear.

'Oh Lord! Lemme go now, non!'

'When I was eighteen years, I had you, Nadie. Eighteen. Eighteen! Eighteen years old is no age for anybody to have little girl! That was *my* mistake. I was too busy with life! I don't want you to make that kind of mistake.'

Nadie looked at the floor. Even the other Nadie was silent.

'You listening, Nadie?'

'Yes, Mai.' Nadie pulled in her lips, biting them on the

inside and keeping her head down so that Mai wouldn't see that there were tears in her eyes.

'You getting big now. You have to know that you and little boys not the same. Don't romp and run about with them as if youall is the same kind of people. You not.' Mai took Nadie's plate, scraped off the fish bones into her own, removed the fork, put her own plate on top of Nadie's. 'You're not the same at all. You never see little boys with babies. Little girls, as soon as they reach your age and start to have their periods like you have last week, they could have babies. Imagine! You wasn't ten years yet when you start. And whenever you see that you start to pass blood like that is trouble that begin. You could have a baby now at the drop of a hat!'

Instinctively, Nadie looked towards the corner by the door where Mai's old brown hat for outside in the garden hung droopily on a nail.

'And is trouble that begin,' said Mai. 'You have to give up everything you want to do in life. Everything.' Mai's right fist was under her chin now and she was looking outside at the old house again. Now she looked sideways at Nadie, almost accusingly. 'You understanding me?'

Nadie looked up guiltily. She had managed to push back the tears. 'Yes, Mai.'

'Don't romp with the boys. When you see the men watching you, look away. All of them spell trouble. That is where the trouble lie. They attack you, tell you how you nice, have their way with you, then they leave you with baby and gone. So avoid them. Just avoid them. You understanding me, child?'

'Yes, Mai.'

The other Nadie tried spelling 'm-a-n' to see if it would spell the same as 't-r-o-u-'. But even she was upset, and her heart wasn't in it.

'All right,' said Mai. 'Go and wash you face properly and look decent. I will wash up these things here.' Mai looked outside again. 'This rain look like it falling forever. I wouldn't go up to the shop today at all. Anyway, I sure Miss Ramdeen and them not expecting me with the weather looking like this. They won't have much to do anyway. It won't have a lot of people in the shop today, and school children not around. I will miss the little day's pay, but is you birthday too, so I don't mind the holiday. Go on, Nadie. Go and wash you face.'

Nadie cried the whole time she was washing her face. Splashed the water against her face and cried and splashed and cried some more. Each time she wiped her face with the towel, she found that she was still crying, so she splashed some more. The other Nadie said, 'Stop that, non! Nadie, *stop that*!' But Mai's Nadie just couldn't stop. She went into her bedroom, threw hereself across the bed and sobbed quietly. 'Mai!' she sobbed. 'Mai! Oh gosh, Mai!' Then she stopped calling on Mai and just cried quietly saying, 'Somebody! Somebody! Somebody!' but then afterwards she sobbed again, 'Mai! Oh gosh, Mai! Mai! Mai! Help me! Help me! Help me!'

'Help you do what?' the other Nadie asked in distress.

'I don't know. I don't know. Just help me.' And Nadie lay with her thumb in her mouth, curled up and sobbing. Then she sat up with the tears running down her face and cried again, 'Oh God! Oh Papa God! Oh God, Mai! Help me!' Then, thinking that Mai might call her to do something or come into the room, Nadie dried her tears, sniffing and wiping across under her nose with her hand.

'Nasty,' pronounced the other Nadie. Mai's Nadie sucked her teeth, went back to the bathroom and bathed her face again.

Sniffing, she walked into her mother's room and stood in front of the mirror. She leaned forward, rubbed her fingers under her eyes, trying to remove the evidence of tears. She opened her eyes wide, closed them, opened them again to see if some of the redness was gone. Nadie sniffed, looked carefully at the sides of her eyes to make sure there was no dirt lurking there. Stood back and looked at the whole of herself in the mirror. The puff sleeves of her dress. Her protruding knees. She wet her finger on her tongue and bent forward to wipe her right knee, to get rid of some of that whiteness. Stood up and looked at her round face. Put her hand up and pushed back the thick plait which stood out over her forehead.

'I all right now?' she asked herself. 'I wonder if I all right now?' Nadie could feel the tears trying to come again but she held them off and stood back to look into her eyes. That's when she became aware of the other little girl. Looking just like her, standing just behind her shoulder, slightly to the left. Nadie rubbed her eyes. The girl was still there. Nadie turned quickly; the girl turned too and was facing in the same direction as she was.

'Mai!' Nadie called quietly. 'Mai!'

Mai walked through the door into the room just at that moment.

'It make no sense washing these clothes today,' she said, looking at the clothes in the basket near to the door. She looked at Nadie's face, at her eyes. 'What wrong with you? Why you stand up staring so?'

Mai couldn't see the other little girl, who was still standing there, staring too. Nadie took a step forward; the girl didn't move, and it was as if Nadie walked into her and she disappeared. Nadie looked around. There was no-one but she and Mai. Nadie wasn't even afraid. With a kind of excitement, she realised what had happened. This was the person inside of her who was always talking and laughing with her about things. Wonderingly, Nadie looked at Mai. Did this happen to other people? Did Mai have another Mai? What was she like?

'Mai?' she said questioningly. 'Mai?'

'What?'

'Nothing.' Nadie turned towards the mirror, stood looking at her face.

Mai shook her head. 'You call me straight, straight so to tell me nothing? You sitting on you senses or something?

Nadie giggled. Sat down on the bed and looked at Mai bending over the clothes basket.

'Sometimes when you walking, eh, Mai, you does think suppose you reach the edge of the world and fall off and you just there falling, falling, falling?'

Mai glanced up. She looked at Nadie's intense face, at the half-opened mouth, at the fingers spread as though to help catch the falling person.

Mai giggled. 'Child, you could talk nonsense!' Mai turned back to her examination of the clothes.

'Eh, Mai, you does think that?'

'And she expecting an answer yes! No, Nadie, I doesn't think no stupidness like that. I normal.'

'Well I does think so, Mai.'

Mai chuckled. 'Well, same thing I tell you. *I* normal. I can't vouch for other people.'

'What is vouch?'

'Kind of swear, non. I can't say for certain how other people like youself does feel.'

'So I not normal, then?'

Mai giggled. 'And she looking serious, yes!' Mai stood up, looking at her daughter, her shoulders shaking with laughter. 'I don't know, Nadie,' she admitted. 'Is you that say. I don't say you not normal, but I never hear about other people thinking they might walk off the side of the world.' Mai laughed aloud. 'Well allyou children could think of nonsense.' She looked at Nadie's serious face and tried to smother her laughter. 'The world round, Nadie. Nobody can't fall off the sides. Ent you learn in school the world round?'

'Yes, but Mai,' in her excitement Nadie was bouncing up and down on the bed. 'Mai . . .'

'Stop that, Nadie. You will break the springs in me mattress. Stop it, I say.'

'All right. Mai!' Nadie held up her hands, one out in front of her on either side of her face, fingers spread. Mai looked between them at the dancing black eyes, at the plait stiff like a question mark above the round face, at the half-opened mouth. What now?

'Suppose eh, Mai, suppose you don't really fall off the edge like, eh, but is as if you go under as the world spinning. Because we in space, you know!' finished Nadie triumphantly.

Mai was laughing so much that she rocked back from the basket and remained sitting on the floor. Mai stretched herself full length on the floor, laughing.

'Oh God, I weak!' Mai said, hardly able to speak for laughter.

Nadie frowned, then smiled, then said again, 'Tell me, non, Mai! In truth.'

'Nadie,' Mai said, sitting up and wiping her eyes, 'whenever they discover this thing you talking about there, whenever it happen to somebody, I will sure write the President or the Prime Minister or the King or the Queen or whoever and tell them,' Mai giggled and wiped at her eyes again, 'tell them that they only *think* they bright, but my little girl was the first person to discover that.'

Nadie laughed with Mai. She was laughing so hard.

'Yes, child. I say you have a important future in front of you, but nothing to say, you starting well early.'

Nadie sucked her teeth, and flung herself across the bed.

'So Mai you never feel as if you are two different people?'

Mai chuckled, and then she was kind of serious. And then she sucked her teeth. And then she chuckled again. 'Sure. A lot of people feel that. And you,' Mai laughed, 'you could be about ten people for all I know. Not all this funny question you does ask there!'

'But Mai is not as if is another person you could see?'

Mai laughed again. 'I doesn't see mine, but who know with youall Gemini people? You're a twin, so you might see yours, yes.' Mai bit her lip, still laughing.

'Oh yes, Mai!' Nadie was on her feet now, standing in front of Mai. 'That is my sign, ain't it? My star sign!'

'Your birth sign, yes. I always hear youall are a strange set of people, and it look so in truth. All this nonsense you talking there, you might well see you Gemini twin in truth,'

Mai chuckled.

'True, Mai?'

'Look, child! Enough nonsense for one morning!' Mai asked suddenly, 'Nadie, where you panties? Clothes here for a whole week of wearing and not one pantie from you. Where them? You wash them? I always telling you to wash them when you bathing, but it would be a miracle if you do that! And I never see no pantie on the line. Where them?' Mai looked at Nadie's face. 'What you squinging away youself looking as if you swallow you tongue for? Raise up you dress let me see what you wearing. Nadie, you wear one pantie for the whole week then? People does bathe and put back on dirty pantie? Come, come let me examine you. So if you fall in the road I have to fraid to come and claim you then? Come, child, let me see if you smell like the drain outside!'

'Ay! What do Mai? Me pantie clean, yes.'

'What do Mai? Come here, child!'

'Well, Mai! How you could just raise up me dress so?'

'So, if this pantie clean, where those dirty ones?'

Mai was on her feet, heading towards Nadie's room. Nadie ran ahead of her, through the door.

'So, Nadie,' Mai stood in the open doorway, looking at Nadie as she held the upturned edge of the mattress, 'you collecting dirty panties under you mattress? You planning exhibition?'

Nadie giggled, knowing that if it hadn't been her birthday she would be in a whole lot of trouble.

'Look child, take that armful of nastiness into the bathroom this minute and start a thorough washing, eh!'

'But, Mai, it raining; how they will dry?'

'You taking chances with me today, you know!'

'No, Mai.'

'Take the sheet out of you mouth; if you hungry go in the kitchen and get something to eat! I don't care if is the flood that on and you have to dive to find the panties and then take them inside Noah's ark to dry, get you tail out there and wash them!' Mai stood back, pushed the door open, and motioned

Nadie towards the bathroom.

'Yes, Mai.' Nadie edged out, and didn't even get a cuff thrown at her. Jesus! Birthdays!

'Wash them good and clean and then hang them up on the line inside the bathroom there. And don't have no water dripping all over the place either. Well I ask you! You ever hear about scientist standing up inside their globe or wherever they does stand up with dirty panties?'

Nadie thought of her general science book. She giggled when she found herself wondering whether those big-time scientists wore dirty underpants.

'Stay inside there laughing as if you think is joke I making with you. You wouldn't learn to have pride in youself at all! I don't understand. Who you take that from?'

And Gemini whispered, 'Must be the good-for-nothing father.'

Nadie could tell that she would have heaps of fun with Gemini. And she did. And sometimes Gemini just made her feel good, and helped her not to be so afraid of people. Once, when she was thirteen and the class giggled at the sight of her name meaning 'nobody' in the Spanish book, Gemini sat down beside her, making Nadie move over to the right edge of the chair so she could have some space, and whispered, 'Don't take them on! Watch that one over there with he big eyes! He is people to laugh at people?' But Nadie only peeped briefly at 'that one over there' and put her head down again. 'Don't study them, Nadie,' insisted Gemini, 'them is folks too? What they know bout "nadie"? They doesn't even get their geometry right!'

'True, yes, true!' And although Nadie didn't answer the taunts, she was able to hold her head up at that thought.

Or sometimes when Nadie reached the bottom of the hill on her way from school and her heart started to beat fast at the sight of the boys on the bridge, Gemini would appear and walk with her. The boys always teased.

They shouted, 'Nadie? Nadie darling? Talk to me, non!'

'Nadie, sugar. I will give you a night you will never

forget!'

'Nadie, love. What you holding it for?'

'Nadie, come let me give you the ting that the doctor order.'

They sang her name. 'Nadie! Nadie sweets?'

They did this, too, when the other girls passed. Sometimes Nadie was with them, or just behind them, or just in front of them, and she always marvelled at the way the girls, even Bianca, would just toss their heads and shout out something like, 'Boy find youself!', or 'Boy find you companion!', 'Boy wash out you mouth when you addressing me!' They sounded just like Gemini. Gemini shouted things like this, too, although only Nadie could hear her. But Nadie just scuttled past with her head down, feeling stupid, as if they were looking at her alone when they shouted.

The young men threw back their heads and laughed and shouted again. And sometimes Nadie's schoolmates brushed their skirts at them, shouting, 'Shoo, fly, don't bother me!'

'Yes,' Gemini sang, 'allyou face like mash potato, go find you companion, boy!' But Nadie kept her head down, or sometimes so high that she stumped her toe in the road and made the men laugh harder.

'Is just a joke, Nadie,' Bianca, who had remained her friend even through high school, said to her one day. 'You too serious. Just laugh at them. Don't study them. Is just jokes. It don't mean nothing.'

One day, when she was walking alone and three young men were standing at the bridge, they didn't tease. One of them left the others and came towards her. He smiled and bowed. Nadie looked at him with wide eyes and said, 'Good afternoon.'

'You going home?' he asked, falling into step beside her.

'Where the backside you think I going?' asked Gemini.

'Yes', said Nadie.

'You always so quiet?'

'You don't know nothing, boy! Hush you mouth!' said Gemini.

Nadie said nothing.

'You don't remember me?'

'Lord, God! What he trying now?' said Gemini.

Nadie glanced quickly, sideways, at him. 'No,' she said hesitantly.

'I came by the house with your uncle one day. My name is Jeffrey. Remember? I used to go to the technical school in town. I left last year.'

Nadie remembered him now. He and Uncle Dan had sat on the stone outside talking and Nadie had watched them through the window. He wasn't so old, really. He was younger than Uncle Dan, who was younger still than Mai. About . . . about . . . well, not old anyway.

'Oh, yes!'

'What you do in school today?'

Gemini sighed. Nadie shrugged. She wondered what the boys on the bridge were thinking. They might be saying something like 'Jeffrey trying to check the thing!' Or 'Jeffrey trying to get a little piece, boy!' She had heard them talk like that, and she knew that they always laughed at girls. Nadie began to feel stupid because she was letting Jeffrey talk to her. Perhaps he was laughing inside himself! She glanced quickly at him. He was smiling a nice, quiet smile at her. Nadie walked faster. But Gemini looked sideways at him and sized him up and said, 'Make you play, boy! What you wasting me time for? Say what you want to say and go you way!'

Jeffrey bent to pick up a stick. He straightened, hit at the bushes at the side of the road with it as he loped along beside Nadie. There were some people walking towards them. Nadie moved quickly to the other side of the road, so that people wouldn't think that she and Jeffrey were walking together. Suppose Mai heard! Gemini looked at them and thought, 'Allyou mouth ready to run! Go and tell Mai! Allyou don't even know what you seeing but you mouth ready to run!'

Just before Nadie turned in to her gap, Jeffrey stopped and said, 'Okay, eh, Nadie! I will see you another time, eh! Take

care of yourself. And stay sweet. You are a really nice girl.'
Nadie couldn't help it. She smiled. That made her feel good.
And Gemini, too, thought, 'Now that ain't so bad. I kind of
like that. All right!' Jeffrey smiled back.

'Okay!' said Nadie.

And then when she turned in to the gap, Mai was there.
And Mai had seen her. Mai had both hands on her hips and
her face was thunder. Nadie's steps slowed.

'Evening, Mai.'

'So, madam, big you start to get big, you not even fourteen
years good yet, you walking bold, bold in the road with man,
bringing them right up to me gap. You playing you tail hot?
Well I will show you who is woman this day!'

'Mai . . .'

'I don't want to hear anything. I talk to you. I explain to
you. I tell you soft, I tell you hard. I speak to you in whisper,
I shout to you; I warn you, and still you taking little man put
on you account. Nadie, you break my heart. Ent I tell you
man mean you no good?'

'Mai, I didn't do nothing, non.'

'You didn't do nothing! I didn't do nothing, she tell me!
You walking in the road smiling up into man face as if is you
husband, Nadie, and then you telling me you didn't do
nothing? My heart grieve to see you, Nadie. When man
smiling for you is time to run, chile; that not nothing good.'

'Mai . . .'

'Go inside.'

'Mai . . .'

'Go inside, I say, and go to you room.'

'Mai . . .'

'I don't want to hear nothing no more, Nadie. I waste
enough talk on you. I tell you, eh, you hurt me heart!'

Nadie sat on her bed and cried. She lay down, turned her
face to the wall, pulled up her knees, put her thumb in her
mouth and cried. 'Mai,' she cried, 'oh God, Mai! Mai! Mai!'

'Don't take her on,' said Gemini. 'That is not nothing to
take on, Nadie. What you crying for? Mai just thinking ting,

but you *know*! Don't take that on. What you crying for? Because you hurt Mai heart? What about *your* heart? Don't take that on, Nadie.' Nadie closed her eyes and sobbed herself to sleep.

A woman body is a dangerous thing, Mai always said, and man is full of wiles. Nadie began to think that she had to be more careful of her body. She admitted that she had actually been pleased when Jeffrey complimented her. As if she didn't know that is because Jeffrey had his plans for her! You forget youself you find youself running fast downhill and you don't know what hit you until you land up at the bottom on you face with all you nose bleeding. Mai had warned her from time. Nadie avoided Jeffrey.

'Girl you stupid!' said Gemini. 'If the man nice he nice regardless of what Mai say! Except you don't think he nice. So is Mai he want to talk to, then?'

'Is not Mai, non. Is me, yes. I want to finish me schooling, yes.'

'So what wanting to finish you schooling have to do with thinking Jeffrey nice? Talk to him, non! When he see you he doesn't even join in with those other boys!'

'Only when he see me! Otherwise he there with them thick, thick!'

'So what? I ain't say he doesn't do and say a lot of thing you don't like, but if he know you mind, Nadie! Think bout that! All them curse you does curse! He would wonder who he talkin too!'

'But not like he! I not like he at all! He only stand up on the bridge with them boys and shouting down women!'

'True. That not nice! Who say that nice? But . . . Look, eh, Nadie, do what you want, but I find he kind of nice. If you are Miss Perfect and he is Mister Bad, go you way. But why you can't be he friend? Talk to him and curse him straight if you want. Instead of cursing him in secret. And . . . Anyway, *I* like him. Do what you want.'

Nadie sucked her teeth, and made sure that she waited for a lift home most times so that she didn't have to walk past the bridge. When she had to, she tried to get company and walk by in a crowd. Then one day she heard one of Jeffrey's friends say to him as she approached. 'Look the thing, boy!' It was the last time Nadie looked Jeffrey's way. She didn't speak to him again. Gemini sighed and was silent.

Nadie began to wonder how to make love and not get pregnant. She didn't know the details. Not that she wanted to, but just in case. Gemini didn't know either.

'Ask Mai!' Gemini said one day.

'How you mean ask Mai! You feel I tired live or something?' Nadie was sitting at table, going through the pages of her biology book, seeing and not seeing. The circulatory system! The sex organs! But how did it happen for real?

'Well how else you expect to know? Ask you friends and them then! Ask Bianca!'

'Bianca? We don't talk so good these days. And she will wonder what I doing. Suppose she start to talk bout me! I can't ask nobody!'

'But Nadie you not living on nobody eyelash! You know Mai always saying let people talk if that give them enjoyment! What you have to fraid what people say for? Sit down there and never do nothing because you fraid people!'

Nadie sucked her teeth, bit her nails, looked over towards the corner. Mai *still* kept an old hat hanging on the nail in the corner.

'Well don't do nothing, then.'

'They not worth it anyway. Is only one thing they want.'

'Lordy!'

Sometimes for weeks Nadie didn't talk to Gemini. She just sulked and ignored her.

Once, when Nadie was nineteen, she *almost* found out the answer to what she had asked Gemini. She had just started working, filling out and stamping forms at the post office. Carlyle, who worked at the post office too, took her out dancing. She didn't let him pick her up at home; but afterwards it was late and he took her home; drove her home in his brother's car. They drove through the trees and Nadie looked up occasionally when she caught a glimpse of yellow as the moon played hide and seek with the car through the trees. Once, Carlyle put out his hand and held hers. Nadie thought, 'Oh Gad! What going on now?' And Gemini chuckled. And the moon peeped.

And then, when he stopped at her house, just behind the fence, Carlyle kissed her. Nadie giggled and pulled away. Carlyle pulled her back to him and kissed her again. Nadie liked it. *Really* liked it. And Gemini said, 'That nice, boy! I ain't joking, non! It great!' Nadie held Carlyle and could feel his hands exploring her body. Worst of all, she could feel her body going downhill. Hurtling fast. Nadie pulled away, whispering 'No.' She was sure that Mai was awake. Mai always said that when Nadie went out she couldn't sleep until she got back. Gemini whispered, 'Dammit to hell you not no little child so what happen if Mai awake?'

And then Nadie said to Gemini, 'But hell I don't know what to do! Should I ask him if he have anything? At least I know that there's something he could wear. How the hell I reach this age and so ignorant about sex? Lord God, what to do? Oh God, Mai, what to do?'

'Mai, hell!' whispered Gemini. 'Do you thing and forget bout Mai!'

'But suppose I get pregnant, Gemini?'

And then Carlyle whispered, 'You want us to go down by the bay and watch the moonlight, Nadie?' And when she didn't answer but still stayed close to him, he continued, 'You using anything, Nadie? I have something.'

Man! Man already! You hear him? Nadie pulled away. Abruptly opened the door of the car.

'Nadie! What's the matter?'

Nadie walked swiftly. How could she let him know? He expected that she knew these things. How could she let him know that she didn't? And you hear him? Telling her he have something. He come prepared to have his way with her. Man already!

'Nadie!' Nadie didn't answer.

'Oh Lord!' said Gemini. 'I give up. Such a nice man. You acting as if he is alone that did want to do thing! Think bout that kiss, non, girl! Oh Lord!'

Mai was furious. Furious that Nadie drive up to her door in man car and sit outside there whispering and behaving like a slut. 'After all I do to give you an education, Nadie! After all I do to see you grow up decent! After how I sacrifice meself! I give up me life to you and that is how you pay me back?'

'I didn't do nothing, Mai! I didn't do nothing, non!'

Mai slapped her that night. Lifted her hand and swiped Nadie across the face. 'You big now. You are you own woman! You working for you money now! You pass exam and have certificate, so you important now! But is me that make you! You never too big for me to lift you and throw you outside the window if I want to! All you doing is making me shame of you! I tell you, I could close me eyes in shame!'

Nadie went to her room, sat on her bed and wept. Held her face in her hands and wept. Deep sobs that clogged up her chest and made her cough.

'You know something, Nadie?' Gemini said thoughtfully, 'I wish I could say I sorry for you, but I not.'

Nadie sobbed harder.

'Seriously. When you were small, was one thing. But not now. If Mai want to throw you out the window, let her throw you, non. Come. Watch outside the window there! It not so high. You could jump. Watch the flower beds that Mai make neat, neat outside there, right under you nose hole. You could jump that easy! Jump and go you way! Tell Mai to rest, non!'

'Gemini! Is only because she love me! Oh God, Gemini! Oh Lord! Is only because she care about me!'

Gemini sighed.

'I don't know what to do! I don't know what to do!'

'That is the problem! You don't know what the hell you want to do! You don't even know if you want to make love to Carlyle in truth. But you probably right. Sit down there and try to do everything the way Mai want it because she love you!'

'Carlyle must be think I really stupid.'

'To France with Carlyle! Let him think what he want! He kissing nice, yes, but so what? To ass was he! What *you* think, Nadie? What *you* really want? So now you thinking about doing everything the way some man want? What *you* want?'

'I don't know.' Nadie put her hands over her face. 'Oh God! Help me! Help me!' she sobbed.

Gemini walked about the room raging. Walked, picked up the hairbrush on the shelf, looked at it, put it back down again. Walked, pounded her fist against the window-pane, looked up at the ceiling, walked again. Walked and sat down on the bed. When Nadie lay curled with her thumb in her mouth, Gemini stood at the window looking out at the moon.

'Look at that star up there, Nadie. Look at that star up there near to the moon. It always there. It close, you know, but still it far away. It not letting the moon suck it in, you know.'

'I'm asleep.'

'You don't have to tell me, sweetheart. You don't have to tell anybody.' Nadie turned during her sleep, and the moon was shining on her face. Right through the window. Then the clouds came and covered the moon. The dogs howled in the night. The cats kept crying like babies. Nadie turned again, and her back was to the window.

People congratulated Mai on the way that she had brought up Nadie.

'God be praised, child. You alone, eh. No help from anybody.'

'Me alone and God, yes. Me alone and God.'

'Give God the praise, child. Give God the praise. You *must* feel good.'

Everyone said that Nadie wouldn't let no little boy twist round her head. A tribute to the loving care of the mother. God don't sleeping, non; he does only pretend he sleeping sometimes give man a chance to form he fashion. He not sleeping at all.

At twenty-three, Nadie was still carrying around the terrible secret not only that she had never slept with any man but that these days she didn't really feel sufficiently attracted to anyone to want to do so. Only Gemini knew. She still met Bianca occasionally, when she came home on holiday from her studies abroad. Bianca had two little girls now. Bianca was noisy and full of fun. One day, sitting on the verandah, she looked at Nadie curiously. 'Why allyou don't move that old house from out there?' she asked. 'Is true the board not rotting. Them old wood so strong, but pull it down, non!' Nadie shrugged. 'What about you, Nadie? How you doing?'

'I there!'

Bianca laughed. 'Girl is either you not doing anything at all or you doing a whole heap and keeping it damn secret! Who is you man, Nadie?'

Nadie sucked her teeth. Bianca leaned across and slapped her on the shoulders. Nadie winced. 'Don't touch me!' she screamed inside. She just didn't like it when people touched her. Anybody!

Nadie began to feel that she had to like *someone*! Why couldn't she get on with people? Once, enjoying a meal with one of her male co-workers, she had seen him signal a negative to an acquaintance at another table. The man had obviously asked him a silent question, with a signal towards her, a lift of the brow or something. Nadie knew the language. 'No,' her companion said. 'Vacant.' Nadie kept looking at her plate, pretended not to understand.

The man approached their table. Sat down with an over-polite 'hello' to which Nadie grunted a response without looking up from her plate.

'The soup nice,' said Gemini, 'but it that nice?' Nadie could feel the man's eyes on her face, assessing, considering. Gemini said, 'No, this one too much. Man go you way, non.' Nadie kept her eyes on her soup.

'Nice,' he pronounced. 'Nice.' And then, looking at her co-worker, 'Unoccupied?'

'Put in your application!' laughed her companion with a

shrug.

Nadie looked up, consideringly. She thought him ugly, his head big, his eyes protruding. But then she had known what he would look like even before she lifted her head to look at him.

'Why', she asked, 'do you people always imagine you are God's gift to some woman?'

'The chair,' he stumbled, with a half-embarrassed laugh. 'It's the chair I was talking about, you know. Unoccupied.'

'I know. What else?'

That time, Gemini had agreed with her. 'Ass-hole,' she said.

Nadie wondered how to form a relationship with someone who considered you a thing. How to start? She watched the men, married or otherwise, assessing women with their eyes, and wanted only to keep away from them.

Once, a man whom she remembered vaguely as one of the boys in her class at primary school told her that he had always admired her. That he liked her still.

'But the boys and them wondering now if is not woman you like,' he said. 'We doesn't see you with no man.'

Nadie looked at him in surprise. 'No,' she said finally. 'No. You mean . . .?' Nadie frowned. 'I never thought about that,' she said. 'I just never thought about that.' Her mind paused. 'I . . .' Now she felt she had to explain why she didn't like him, why she didn't want him as a lover. 'Is just that I think men . . . well . . . most of those *I* meet anyway, talk about women as if they are . . . well . . . I just don't like it. As if, we are *things*! And always want to check every woman they see! And . . .'

'Oh come on, Nadie. If a fella see a nice piece o ting, he going check it, and that is all. What you mean bout checking every woman? Allyou woman just gettin a whole heap of foreign ideas these days!'

And Nadie walked away.

Mai, too, was beginning to get concerned. 'Nadie,' she said one day, 'you never bring a young man to me to say well this is my young man or anything. Is about time for you to settle down.'

Nadie smiled. 'I have no-one I interested in, Mai.'

'Well you have to look out for youself. You have to see about your future, child. Me, I starting to go downhill now; the years coming on. You have to look out for yourself.'

'Well!' said Gemini, 'is the first time I hear that years does bring people downhill too! All this time I thought was only man! Nadie, tell her to leave you alone let you work out you life, eh!'

'Is Mai you talking about, you know, Gemini!'

Gemini sighed. 'That is the problem,' she agreed. 'Is Mai.'

'You know, Mai? I think you were right all the time. The men not worth it. They think very little of women. I can't see anyone . . .'

'Child, it must have somebody. And sometimes you have to take the good with the bad and make the most of it.'

Nadie laughed. 'Mai, you not easy, you know that? You just not easy!'

'Is not a joke, child.'

'No, Mai. Is not a joke.'

Nadie met Butter at Mai's workplace one day. She strolled into the shop to speak to Mai and there he was leaning against the counter. Nadie glanced at him only for as long as it was necessary to frame a greeting. But then Mai said, 'Bertrand, this is my daughter Nadie. Nadie, this is Miss Ramdeen's nephew.'

'*Adopted* nephew, if such a thing exists,' he laughed, extending his hand. 'She's actually my godmother and acts as mother, aunt, everything in one. Even when I'm miles away.'

'Your mother's alive?'

'Oh yes! Very much so. Aunty's a second mother.'

'Oh!' said Nadie. And Gemini said, 'Nice voice.'

'Nadie!' said Bertrand. 'Nice name. Nice *sounding* name, that is, if we look at it from the standpoint of the English language. But actually it's not very flattering in Spanish, is it?'

Nadie sighed. 'It isn't. I'm exactly no-one, am I not?' Nadie glanced in the direction of her mother, but Mai was busy attending to customers.

'Don't worry,' grinned Bertrand. 'It's better than Butter.'

'How do you mean?'

'I'm Butter.'

'Butter?'

'Officially Bertrand. But thanks to the language peculiarities of a baby brother long ago, nobody calls me anything but Butter. I've tried to shake it off, but it usually comes back to haunt me.'

Nadie laughed. 'I've never tried to shake off Nadie, really. But I do tend to think of myself as Gemini,' Nadie startled herself by saying. And she distinctly heard Gemini chuckle.

'Why Gemini?'

'My birth sign.'

'You believe in such things?'

Nadie shrugged.

Butter walked home with her that day. They talked and laughed easily and were actually sitting on the steps shouting with laughter when Mai came home. Butter was telling her about himself, about his brother who had left home and hearth to live in the hills, about how he himself went sometimes to 'hang out' for a few nights with his brother. About his sometimes job for a foreign company which dug up archaeological remains of the Caribs and Arawaks to send to some museum in New York. About the questions he asked about life. And he *listened* to what she had to say. Asked her questions.

'So you couldn't take Butter inside, Nadie?'

'The steps all right, Mai. We all right.'

'We're fine here, Mai,' Butter agreed.

Nadie talked to Butter as she had never talked to anyone but Gemini before. Butter even told her that sometimes he felt he was two people, that she would be surprised if she could read the things his mind wrote sometimes, especially when he was writing up his report for the museum. Sometimes, too, he called her Gemini, and Nadie smiled.

Nadie didn't mind it when Butter touched her. She didn't mind it at all. She ignored Gemini who commented that it was strange that she was suddenly able to find out where gynaecologists were and what forms of contraception to use. Marvelled that lovemaking was suddenly so tender and so beautiful and that men could really be so caring.

Butter loved music and would sit holding Nadie's hand and talking about music. He talked about the dances in his village in Carriacou and showed her how he danced then. Sometimes she wanted to dance with him when he did that, but was afraid that he would watch her. So she let Gemini dance. Butter couldn't see except when she became Gemini for him. And sometimes Butter looked at her curiously, as though he wondered why she wouldn't dance. Once he visited her with a drum and taught her to play some rhythms. He talked about his mother. He talked about his grandmother. He talked about his own attitudes to women and how sometimes these were so bad.

And Gemini said, 'Now *that* is man. This one not man pattern. That is *man!*'

And Nadie agreed. 'Yes. He kind of nice. In fact, he really nice. I watching him, but he really nice.'

Then one day when Nadie and Butter were on the beach together, he introduced her to a friend. She saw the look the two exchanged, saw the friend's eyebrows go up, heard Butter's easy laugh. Later, as she lay on the sand with her eyes closed, she heard their conversation.

'Nice piece o beef, man. Where you get it?'

And Butter *laughed*. 'Up by me aunt and them, man.'

'It nice, man.'

'Well, you know me. I does go in for the best.'

'So what bout the ting round the corner by me there?'

'I have that under control still, man. Things cool.'

'I thought you and that one did heading for the church, you know.'

'Boy what do you? You see me, man. I know woman. Give them a little, little inch so and they want to take a whole mile. Just keep them guessing. That is the best way to control them. Man, we know this kind of thing from since we growing up. You stupid or what?'

'Nastiness!' said Nadie, turning over to bury her face in the sand, feeling suddenly stupid and small. 'Damn nastiness!'

'Hold on!' said Gemini. 'Tell him what you hear if you want, and tell him not to play the ass! But don' take that on! All of that is mouth. You know how them men stop already. They just have to be big and tough.'

'Nastiness!'

'I agree. A damn nastiness in truth; but that is small potatoes, girl!' Gemini laughed. 'Throw that over you shoulder. The man enjoying heself. He like you, but he have ting in he skin, too! If you could deal, deal! And juk him in he skin sometimes, don't let him take you and tie rope, but don't take that make youself get ulcer! Forget bout he, or deal as you want to deal, but what you gettin ulcer for? What does happen to you sometimes?'

Nadie raged and cried. She watched Butter closely and cried every time she thought that he was just the kind of nastiness Mai used to talk about. She stopped really talking to Butter, stopped telling him things, except when something really upset her and she watned to hear what he thought about it, like if something happened at the post office. Because one thing with Butter, he could listen. 'He really good, you know!' she said to Gemini. And Gemini said, 'Well, *one* of him!'

And while Nadie was still thinking about that and wondering if she liked him in truth, one day Butter told her that if she didn't think he could give her what she wanted in life, she should find someone else. Just like that. He just sort of lifted his shoulders and said it. Not that he didn't care something about her, he said, but, that was life. That was when Nadie began to be afraid to touch him. To be afraid that when she touched him he was really flinching inside as she used to do sometimes with Mai. Because of course that was life! You could like and not like at the same time! Did it matter? And she became very still and sort of listening if he made any movement to touch her.

In her room that night, Nadie cried to Gemini. And most of the time she didn't know what she was crying for. She didn't know if she was crying because she loved Butter and he didn't love her, or because she had discovered that she didn't love him after all. She just knew that both Butter and Mai said life was like that, that Bianca had said you mustn't take things too seriously, and that she didn't love or like anybody, really.

'I feel so small! Oh God, Gemini, I feel so small!'

Gemini yawned. Nadie said nothing for a while.

'Don' lecture no big man, Nadie. Even when we in school, we never really like the school bench. If is so you feel, let Butter go he way! Siddown there and wait for man to make you feel good about youself! You feeling small? Nonsense!'

Nadie stood facing the mirror. Looking at her eyes, large, black, fearful. Lips, trembling today, as they often did when she was with Butter these days. Not firm and determined like they were usually, when she was at work, or with most other people. Was Gemini right? Was she strong with everyone except Butter? Did she become weak and stupidee when he was around? So? What was it *she* wanted? The Butter who talked about women as though they were objects? The Butter who used to be tender and loving with her? Or no Butter at all? Which Butter really existed? Did it matter? Nadie's lips trembled. Gemini said, 'Backside! What do this woman?'

Nadie went again to see Butter, tried to get him to convince her that he was not what Mai would call another nastiness, that she hadn't really heard him speak in the way she thought she had, that in any case that was nothing, he didn't mean it. He couldn't really mean it either when he said that she could do as she pleased. Not the way she loved him. 'Or think you do,' said Gemini, who seemed to be slowly going off Butter.

And while Nadie was talking to him, the thought came to her, 'If Mai told me I could do as I pleased, would she really love me?'

And Gemini said, 'Oh Lord!' And when Nadie asked, 'How could you, Butter? How could you be so uncaring?' Gemini hid her face in her lap and moaned, 'Oh Lord, I don't want to see this!'

Nadie told Butter that her criticism only reflected how much she loved him. Gemini sat back and said, 'Jesus Lord, this not happening in truth!' Butter looked bored.

Nadie said, 'You must try to be a different person, Butter. You shouldn't talk that way about women! How could you be so different when you are with me?'

Gemini paced restlessly. 'The school bench uncomfortable for him, Nadie,' she whispered, 'he legs kind of long.' Nadie bent her head and twisted her fingers. She wondered what to do, what to say. She looked up and Butter's eyes were on her. They were calculating, assessing. His mouth was turned up, scornful. His fingers stroked his chin.

'Doesn't he love me any more?' Nadie asked Gemini.

'He tired,' said Gemini, 'Go to ass home, Nadie! The man tired! And to tell you the truth, you should be blâsted tired too! Go to ass home!'

'I need your help, Butter,' Nadie said.

Gemini groaned. 'Oh Jesus!' she said, 'Not that!'

'I need your help to work out so many things. You do so many things to hurt me, and you go so silent I don't know what you're thinking . . .'

'Oh Lord, Nadie!' said Gemini, 'This is not a soap opera, this is life. People don't get on like this. I don't know you. I don't want to know you. Who you be?' Where you does suddenly come from behaving in this kind of way? Why I always feel I know you?'

Some restraining force inside of Butter seemed to step aside. 'Let me tell you something!' he began, and suddenly Nadie didn't want to hear this something.

'The thing is . . .' she began.

'No. Let *me* talk for a change. What about me? I not hurt too? You could never listen to *me*! Your problem is that you think you're the only person in the world!'

He may have said more. He must have said more, because his lips continued moving. Nadie didn't hear any more. You think you're the only person in the world. Nadie looked down at her hands, linked palms facing upwards in her lap. She looked at the deep-brown lines which formed a definite 'N' in her palms. When she looked up, Gemini was sitting directly opposite her, in front of Butter. Gemini said nothing. For the first time, the two stared into each other's eyes.

'It had to come to this, Nadie,' Gemini said quietly. 'You can't go on looking for somebody to give you yourself. You have to go to people *with* yourself.'

And when Nadie didn't answer, Gemini called softly, 'Nadie?'

Still, Nadie remained silent. But she was just looking stunned, not as if she wanted to cry. Not really. Lonely, perhaps, but not weepy.

'Why you looking at me like that?' asked Butter. 'What it is you want to say to me?' And it was as if he wanted to know what she had to say. As if he was puzzled too, and didn't quite know what this was that was happening between them. Why they quarrelled. Why they loved. Why she wouldn't leave him alone! If . . . If . . . and Butter looked down at his hands . . . if that was what he wanted. He thought perhaps it was.

'Nothing,' said Nadie. 'Nothing.'

And suddenly Butter was looking almost as lonely as she was feeling. For the first time, Nadie looked at him and realised that she could say, *chou poule*! What happen, happen. Nadie looked at Butter, thinking of that first day on Mai's step, thinking of the day on the beach, thinking of the way she lectured him. And she thought, I don't know you, and you don't know me either! Truth to tell, Butter, I don't even know myself!

At home that night, Nadie didn't cry. She looked in her mirror and asked, 'Do *I* like myself?' Nadie smiled. Now that's a beginning! Not 'Does Mai like me really? Can I really live up to all that Mai wants?' Not even 'Does Butter like me really?' Do I like myself? Jesus, it take me nearly a quarter of a century to ask that! You think you're the only person in the world.

For the first time that she could remember, Nadie went to bed thinking, What happen, happen? It don't matter. Don't force nothing. Let it ride. Nadie looked up at the window. She must put that curtain up some time. Some time.

The men were there, standing on the left and on the right, at the bottom of River Hill. They shouted as Nadie walked past. She sucked her teeth, laughed and shouted back, 'Know you place!' Then she looked to the left again. Gemini was running towards her, smiling. They linked arms and walked, talking and laughing, up the hill. Then Nadie was walking alone, pointing and shouting, pointing towards the top of the hill, where the mist was clearing. Shouting! Nadie woke with a start, shouting.

It was early morning, and the light was streaming through the window-pane, onto her face. Outside, a bird was singing the early morning song 'Green peas sweet, green peas sweet!' Nadie smiled. Another day had begun.

The Visit

The woman sat leaning slightly forward. Left
elbow on leg, left hand holding up her chin, clamping shut
her lips. Not hiding their look of sullen disinterest. From the
doorway, her daughter watched her. Took in the droop of the
shoulders, the emptiness in the heavy-lidded black eyes.

'You watching that programme?'

Miriam shrugged, not moving her hand, not moving her
eyes from the television. Catherine sighed, leaned in the
doorway and turned her eyes towards the television. Jensen's
Dream! The woman was trying to prevent Jensen from
getting the deal on the plantation. Catherine hoped that he
would find out in time to stop her. She glanced over at her
mother. Lord! Look at her! Just look at her! She had to choose
the most uncomfortable chair in the room, quite in the corner
over there! And look at her face! Anybody come in here and
see her looking like that must think I making her see trouble!
Just look at her! Catherine sucked her teeth and turned away
from the doorway, moving back to the kitchen.

Martin looked up from his job of washing dishes at the
kitchen sink. He chuckled. Stepped back and blocked his
sister's path with his elbow. 'Behave yourself, non!' he said in
a low voice. 'Leave the lady alone!'

Catherine matched his tone. 'Go and watch her! Go and see
how she sit down poor-me-one as if somebody thief she best
clean-neck fowl!'

Martin laughed quietly, the sound staying down in his

throat. He picked up a glass and placed his hands back in the water. 'Behave yourself,' he repeated, 'leave her alone!'

His answer was a prolonged sucking of the teeth as his sister moved towards the refrigerator.

Jensen was confronting his secret adversary. He was beginning to suspect that something not quite right was going on.

Miriam had heard the whispering. Guessed that it had something to do with her. She removed her hand from under her chin, frowned, looked cross-eyed at the door, shifted herself sideways in the chair, crossed her legs and leaned her head cautiously back. Her right ear just touched the cushion.

An advertisement. Some kind of sauce. Miriam didn't hear what sauce it was. A far-off memory came back to her. An advertisement on radio years ago. 'Don't just say Worcester! Say Bee and Digby's!'

Miriam cleared her throat and hunched her shoulders. Couldn't they do something to make it a little warmer? Put on the fire or something? Miriam yawned. She would have liked to go and lie down. Cover up. She smiled. *Kooblay* up! But for sure Catherine would want to know if she was ill or something. Quietly, so as not to be heard, Miriam sucked her teeth and turned in the chair. Her body was curved, head down, her back turned now towards the television.

April in England. Catherine and Martin had said when they wrote that it was a good time to come. Not very hot, but good weather. Springtime! Good weather! Well I wouldn't like to see bad one! Last week, when they had gone to visit Cousin Bertrand in Huddersfield, it had snowed! Miriam shivered. Martin, who wasn't a bad child, really . . . Not like his sister. Is as if she think England is hers and she doing me a favour to have me here! Favour? I want to go home, yes! I want to go home where me is woman in me own house!

Martin said that Huddersfield and that whole area around there was like that. Always cold. Always cold. When there was snow in Huddersfield, he said, it didn't mean that there was snow in London, too. In fact afterwards they knew that it hadn't snowed in London that day. But snow or no snow, it well cold! It well, well cold!

I tell you, eh, it hurting me heart. Catherine! Look at Catherine, non! I remember how I nurse that child! Puny, puny, she did nearly dead, yes! They didn't even think she would survive! And now acting with me like if she think she is queen!

When she had sat there in Peggy's Whim, high up on the hill above Hermitage, writing Martin and Catherine here in England, she never would have thought that England was like this. No. 30 Rose Mansions, Bedford Street, London NW . . . NW . . . either 3 or 5, she could never remember. Those England addresses were so long! Rose Mansions! Rose Mansions! She had expected . . . she had expected . . . well, not a *mansion*, but something different to this. This high, high building, all the markings on the wall downstairs, and you had to travel up in a dark, dark elevator! Like a hole! And even those steps! Miriam lifted her head, turned, looked around her. I mean, when you reach inside here, it not bad. It nice, she conceded. They have the place well put away! Well put away!

Furtively, she looked around the room. The little carpet well nice, the bookcase in the corner well neat, the pictures on the wall, well . . . not my choice, these kind of mix-up colours that you don't even know what you looking at, but is all right. Miriam's eyes moved to the records stacked in the corner, the music set on the side by the television. Everything well put away! Is to be expected. Both of them know from time how to take care of a place. They didn't grow up anyhow, if even self we was poor. Her eyes travelled around the room. She looked down at the corners. The place clean. The place well clean. Catherine could work. I know that. And Martin never had nobody servanting for him. He accustom cooking and looking after himself. He spend enough time looking after the house and seeing after Catherine while I go to work! So they all right. They could see after theyself from time!

But . . . Miriam looked around the room again, sucked her

teeth softly, leaned her head back against the cushion. So this England is place to live too, then? Only coop up, coop up inside a house all the time? Miriam sucked her teeth again, too loudly this time.

'You all right, Mammie?' Catherine asked from the doorway, unbuttoning her jeans at the waist to ease the pressure.

'Yes,' Miriam answered in an almost questioning tone, a resigned sort of tone that infuriated Catherine. 'Yes, I all right, yes.'

'Well Mammie, how you doing *kabusé, kabusé* so? As if you seeing trouble?' Miriam sniffed, held on to the arms of the chair and drew herself to a more upright position. 'Why you sit down there in the chair looking poor-me-one, poor-me-one so? Lively up yourself, non!'

'Madam Catherine, if you don't want me to sit down in you chair, just tell me, yes. I not beggin nobody for a cup of water, non! I have me house, yes. I didn't ask allyou to come up here. So I could pack me things and go whenever allyou ready! All I will ask you is to drop me on the airport please. And even self you don't want to do that, I sure I could find me way. I not beggin nobody for a drop of water, non! I could go back home in me house this evening self, self!'

Martin pushed past his sister, walked towards his mother, laughing. 'So who is allyou now?' he asked. 'Who you cursing in smart there?' He sat on the arm of the chair, hugged her, leaned his head against hers.

'You smell of onion, boy! Don't try to mamaguy me at all! Move away from me!'

'Come on, Mums. Don't take things so hard.' He put his other arm around her. Catherine grumbled something and moved back into the kitchen.

'I want to go home, yes,' said Miriam. 'Youall just drop me on the airport let me find me way, please. I don't want to come in people place come and give them trouble!'

'Mum, why you acting as if you with strangers? How you mean in *people* place come and give them trouble? Who is this *people*?'

'I don't have time bandy words with you and you sister, non! I . . .'

'My sister? You daughter, yes! Come on, Mums!'

He shook her gently. 'Is just a short holiday. Relax and enjoy yourself. You're so tense up! Is only because Catherine wants to see you happy. You just sit there looking so sad, hardly eating . . . How you think we feel?'

'I not trying to make youall unhappy, so let me go where I happy. I don't like this place. It cold, cold; you can't move; if it little bit bright, which is hardly, and I want to take a walk outside, I have to say where I going, as if me is some little child; I have to ring doorbell to annoy people for them to let me in again . . . How people could live like that? In a house, in a house all day long?'

'Mums, that's the way it is here. And it's more difficult because we have to be running around, getting Carl to school and to the baby-sitter; we couldn't take our holidays same time, so I have to be rushing off to work sometimes; it's different! But it's just a short holiday! Enjoy yourself! We want to see you feeling happy! And look, you even have a chance to meet your grandson for the first time!'

'That self is another thing. Perhaps you should have send that child home for me since after the mother dead. The two of you letting him do exactly what he want. The child talking to you just as he want, saying what he feel? No. Is not so. Is so England children is, then? No wonder it have so much bad thing happening all over the place!'

Martin removed his arms. Linked his fingers, unlinked them and leaned towards the small table to pick up the remote control for the television.

'You not watching that, non?'

'What?' His mother's eyes followed the direction of his glance. 'No. No. I not watching no television!'

Martin pressed a button on the control. The image faded. 'Carl's all right, Mum. He's doing pretty well at school and . . . I encourage him to express his ideas.' He leaned forward again, put down the control, sat looking at the photograph of his son on the side table. Carl was holding a ball, looking straight into the camera, his tongue out. That had been taken last summer, up on Hampstead Heath. Carl was wearing a T-shirt and shorts. Martin's long face was serious, thoughtful, as he watched his son's laughing face. He turned his eyes towards his mother's face. 'Carl's a fine child, Mums.'

'Papa, take care of allyou children as allyou want, you hear. Is your responsibility. I just want to go where I living!'

'You only have two more weeks, Mum.'

'If you could organise it for me to leave before, I will be very grateful.'

Martin hunched his shoulders. Cracked his fingers. 'Okay,' he said. 'Okay, Mum. Whatever you want.' He sat there a while longer, then stood up and moved back towards the kitchen.

I know he feeling bad, but I just don't like this place! Not me and England at all! After a while, Miriam pushed herself up from the chair and walked slowly out to the kitchen.

'We're almost finished,' Martin said.

'Nothing I could do?' Miriam asked.

Catherine turned from taking something off a shelf. Picked up the jug of juice. 'Just put this juice on the table for me, Mammie. And if you want, while I setting the table, you could take out those clothes in the washing machine and hang them up in the bathroom.'

'All right.'

It had started from the time she reached the airport here, really. Before that, Miriam had been excited about the visit. It was only when she reached Heathrow that she started feeling perhaps she should have stayed at home.

Walking up in that line and waiting to go to one of those customs officers. Was customs, non? Customs, or immigration, or something. One of them. Just standing in that line she had remembered school, all those donkey years ago. Standing in line for the ruler from Teacher Alfred. And that man was a beater! She remembered a day when she didn't know all of her poem. She could even remember the book! Royal Readers,

Book . . . Book . . . She couldn't remember which number
Royal Readers, but it was Royal Readers, anyway. And the
lesson was

> *Lives of great men*
> *All remind us*
> *We can make our lives sublime*
> *And departing leave behind us*
> *Footprints on the sands of time*

> *Footprints that . . .*

And that's the part that she had forgotten. Standing in line at
Heathrow airport, Miriam realised that she *still* couldn't
remember it.

Standing taking clothes out of the washing machine, she
didn't remember it still. Miriam laughed at herself, out loud.
Said, 'Well yes, wi!' Catherine and Martin exchanged glances.

The man at the airport desk had asked a lot of questions.
And Miriam had started to feel guilty. She didn't know why,
because she didn't have anything to hide. But she had felt
really guilty. It was as if he thought she was lying about
something.

'You say your daughter and son invited you here on this
holiday?'

Miriam had cleared her throat, put her hand to her mouth,
said, 'Sorry!' Inclined her head slightly. 'Yes, sir.'

'And this here; this is the address you're going to?'

'Yes, sir!'

'What does your daughter do?'

'She's a teacher, sir.'

'Your daughter is a teacher in this country?'

He had looked up at her then, lifting his eyebrows questioningly.

So what the hell? You think I can't have a teacher daughter
here? 'Yes, sir.'

He kept her waiting while he looked through her passport

again. There was nothing to see. She had only travelled to
Trinidad on it before. Many times. To sell things in the
market there. And to Barbados once. He seemed to examine
each stamp. Then he picked up her ticket. Examined that,
too.

'Will your daughter be here at the airport to meet you?'

'Yes, sir.'

'You'll be here for three weeks?'

Well look at the flicking ticket, non! 'Yes, sir.'

Finally, he had looked up at her and his eyes seemed to say,
'Well, I guess I'll let you go through, even though I'm sure
you're lying.' His lips didn't say anything more. He stamped
her passport.

By the time Miriam had got through customs and walked
out to find Catherine, Martin and Carl, Martin's six-year-old
son, waiting for her, she was near to tears. Something that
hadn't happened for a long time. Her shoulders were hunched
and she was feeling as small as Cousin Milton's little Maria
back home; Maria who usually stayed with her in Peggy's
Whim.

She had felt strange with her children and grandson from
the beginning. She found that she just couldn't laugh and talk
with them as usual. Especially when Carl said, 'You're my
nan?' And she started off wondering why he had said it like
that.

And then she found that Carl wasn't like a child at all. He
asked big people questions, talked all the time, and Catherine
and Martin just wouldn't shut him up. That must be England
style. They didn't grow like that at all.

And Miriam's voice began to sound strange in her own
ears, especially when Carl talked to her in that funny accent of
his. It made him sound even more like big people.

Two more weeks away! The second of May. Miriam
wondered if Martin would try to get the date changed. She
wouldn't say it again, but she hoped that he would remember.

It rained on April the twenty-seventh. They travelled by

the underground train. Took a taxi to the station, hurried out in the rain, and went with the two suitcases down the escalator to take the Northern line to King's Cross. Then they changed to the Piccadilly line, which went all the way out to Heathrow airport.

At the BWIA airline counter, Miriam began to brighten up. She smiled often. Even seemed to be holding herself back from exploding with laughter. She touched Carl on the head and said 'Young Mister Carl, eh!'

'You must come again, Nan,' Carl said.

'All right, son.' Miriam laughed, glanced at Catherine.

'You know you're only saying that,' said Catherine, leaning across and straightening her mother's collar. 'You didn't like it at all.'

'Well,' Miriam shrugged, still smiling, 'all place have their people.'

'Yes, Madam Diplomat,' said Martin.

Miriam laughed again, leaning back in the way that they remembered. Martin and Catherine looked at each other and shook their heads. Catherine's smile was disbelieving. 'So Mammie you just start to enjoy yourself, then?' she marvelled.

'Child, leave me alone, non. Is home I going, yes.' Miriam touched her daughter's face. 'Don't mind. Don't mind that!'

'Well I never!' said Catherine.

They sat in the airport cafeteria and drank orange juice. 'This orange juice could have do with a little touch of something stronger in it!' laughed Miriam. 'But,' she added with a laugh as they both looked up at her, 'is all right; is all right; I will make do.'

Catherine folded her lips and said nothing. Martin laughed. 'The lady start to enjoy sheself when she going, yes! Yes, Mammie! Ye-e-s! You not joking!'

Miriam leaned back and smiled at her grandson.

'You're nice, Nan,' said Carl, looking at her critically. 'When will you be back?'

'Son, I don't know, non. Is you to come to visit me now!'

'Yes!' said Carl enthusiastically. 'Yes, Nan.' Carl looked from his father to his aunt.

'Don't look at me,' said Catherine. 'That is you and your father's business.'

'Dad?'

'Yes. We'll have to plan it. We're overdue for a visit.'

'Well that is all you'll hear now until the date is set.' Catherine drained her orange juice, leaned across and handed a tissue to Carl. 'Wipe your mouth, Carl.'

The three were quiet as they watched Miriam walk through to emigration. She turned and waved, her round face smiling broadly, the light brown hat that she liked to wear perched almost jauntily on her head, her body looking smaller than when she had first arrived, but her face shining with health and happiness. Martin looked down at his sister. Back at his mother. 'Is now I could see how much you two look alike,' he said. 'Short same way. Same round face. And then both of you stubborn same way.'

Catherine chuckled. 'She not joking in truth, you know.'

'Your mother looking well young, you know, girl.'

They waved again. Miriam disappeared around the corner. Carl shouted, 'See you in Grenada, Nan!'

They stood for a while looking at the wall around which Miriam had disappeared. 'Never me again,' said Catherine, as they turned away. 'Never me again.'

'Never me again,' said Miriam to Cousin Milton the next morning. They were sitting under the tamarind tree on the hill just near to her house. 'You see that little devil?' she asked in a lower voice, looking down the hill towards a boy of about six who was moving backwards, staring at them, finger in his mouth. 'Is me tambran he coming after, you know. See he see us here, he backing back now. But is me tambran he was coming after.'

Cousin Milton glanced at the retreating youngster, turned his attention back to Miriam. 'But girl, how you mean you don't like England, dey? So England is place not to like, then?'

'I don't care what you say!'

'All round you, you seeing England pounds putting up house; all who stay in England for thirty years and more coming back put up house to dead in luxury, you self saying you don't like England? How you mean? Girl, don't talk this thing hard make people laugh at you at all! Keep that to youself!'

Miriam laughed. 'You all right yes, Cousin Milton. Anyway, that is one episode that over! Dead and bury. Not me and England, non. Never me again! Give me me place where I could sit down outside and see people, do what I want. Not me at all. All place have their people! Never me again!'

Milton sighed. Opened his mouth and seemed about to say something. Lapsed into thoughtful silence.

'Never!' pronounced Miriam.

My Sister Cherish

Whenever I think of my sister Cherish, I remember the bird. I saw it on the window-sill of the room a few days after she died. Or was it the day after she died? I was going into the room to get something. I don't remember what. But then I saw the bird, and backed towards the door. A white, long-legged bird, just standing there picking something off the window-sill. Or was it looking towards the bed where Cherish used to lie, looking at the window sometimes and laughing? The bird lifted its head towards the room. I watched it, and backed towards the kitchen. For the rest of that day, I kept as close to my mother as I could, but at fourteen it is not easy to find a reason to be always standing close to one's mother, so I tried to keep her in sight as much as possible. I sat in the dining-room and watched her working in the kitchen. When she hummed or sang, I closed my eyes a little. I stood at the window and watched her when she went to hang the kitchen towels on the line. Perhaps it was partly because it was Sunday that I felt like that, because Sunday was a logical sort of day for spirits to visit. For the whole of that day, the leaves of the trees seemed greener, the breeze blew more gently than usual; even the sun was softer. There was so much tenderness and uncertainty and fear around that even when my brother tried to start a quarrel, I just looked at him and smiled. Mom stopped her humming then and stared at me.

'What wrong with you today? Jumbie got you tongue?'

'Don' say dat, non.'

My mother looked at me, the frown on her forehead reflecting my own. I knew she was watching the light fold of my bottom lip where the lower teeth were worrying the inside of my mouth. She laughed. My mother always did things like that, laughed when someone else was looking really serious about something and she couldn't quite figure out what there was to be so serious about.

'So is true, then? Jumbie have you tongue in truth?' She giggled.

I didn't answer, and my mother went back to her humming of 'How Great Thou Art'. It annoyed me, usually, this Sunday hymn-singing, or hymn-humming, really, since my mother often didn't know the words. She would sing out loud:

> O Lord my God
> When I in awesome wonder
> Consider a-a-all
> The things that thou hast made

And then would come a humming of this same tune again. Afterwards she would hold her head up high and look out of the window – it seemed that she was always near to a window for this part of the song – and sing out loud again, looking at the blue sky with the flecks of white clouds skidding across:

> How great thou a-a-art

and then some more humming, followed by the slow, climactic

HOW GREAT THOU ART!

My mother would stand for a while after this, wringing the towel or wiping her hands or something and just looking out at the sky and the palm tree quiet in the distance. Then she would turn away to do something else in the kitchen, starting to hum again.

That Sunday the singing didn't annoy me. I just listened and felt kind of sad. It wasn't that I was afraid, really. Well, yes it was, in a way, because I tried not to remember what Cherish's face was like as she lay there on the bed day after day. And I looked behind me often. And I looked around the yard to see what sort of birds were there. But . . .

'Mammie, I saw a bird on the window in your room this morning.'

My mother looked at me and waited. When I said nothing further, she frowned, and her mouth opened slightly. I wanted to giggle then, because I could see that she was beginning to wonder if I was going mad. Although I wanted to laugh, I knew it was something that worried my mother every so often. Some time, far back in the family, she had a great-great-grandparent who had gone mad because of worries. My mother was always afraid that this madness would suddenly appear again and claim someone who was having worries. I knew, because she had told me the story, and sometimes when things started to bother her, she would suddenly say, 'Anyway let me don't take on that, eh! We not a family with strong head.' This always sounded strange, because it seemed to me that my mother had the strongest head I knew. I think she worried more about me than anything. Sometimes, if we had just heard about someone who was ill, or sick, and I asked lots of questions about it, she would sound annoyed. Then soon afterwards she would say, 'Take that look outa you eye. Why you stand up there lookin like you in wonderland, so? I tell you already you don't have to take the troubles of the world put on you shoulders. Fix you face, girl!' I didn't say anything more now. I just waited. I knew that my mother would speak again.

'So?'

'It was a white bird, the ones with long, long legs.'

'Galain?'

'I dunno.'

'So what happen if a bird on the window in my room? You know somebody buy spot there?'

'It was a white, white bird, you know, and sometimes when people die . . .'

My mother chuckled. 'So you think might have been Cherish?'

I didn't really know what I thought, so I just stood biting my lip. My mother sat down in the living-room and hummed for a while again, as though she had forgotten about me. This time she was humming 'Jesus Gentlest Saviour'. Then the humming stopped. I watched her turning the pages of her hymn book. She lifted a hand and pushed the glasses further up her nose.

'So that is why you wouldn't go in the room all day?'

I frowned.

'For a person who grow up going to church every Sunday, you really superstitious.'

I just steupsed.

'Who you steupsing for? Don' make me give you one box, eh!'

I didn't say anything, and Mammie stopped looking fierce. She leaned back in the rocking chair and rubbed her feet together.

'But you know, if is you sister spirit, which I doubt,' she chuckled, 'you have nothing to fear. It wouldn't do you anything but good. She gone to the angels for sure. Never do a thing to hurt anybody in her life. For sure she gone to the angels. Spirit like that is good spirit.'

'Don' talk about that, non!'

'So is me that bring up the conversation, then? Girl behave youself, eh!' My mother sucked her teeth and went back to her humming.

Later that evening, I heard her whispering to herself in the kitchen, 'Gone to the angels for sure, God rest her soul.' And then I heard her telling Daddy, 'You daughter think she see her sister spirit on the window in the room.'

Daddy gave an uncertain half-laugh at first. 'Why? What?

What she see?'
    'A bird.'
    'A bird?'
    'Yes. She see a white bird on the window. For the whole day she won't go in the room, and then just afterwards she come telling me about this bird.'
    Daddy chuckled then, the laugh starting deep inside his throat. But I knew from the way he answered at first that he was wondering if I had seen Cherish for real. It sort of made me more frightened, because it meant that my father wasn't so sure that there weren't spirits. Besides, there were times when Mammie would say, 'Ah chuts,' when we talked about someone who had seen a spirit, and Daddy would look as if he agreed with her. But soon afterwards he would start a spirit story beginning, 'But in spite of that, there are things you can't explain, you know. Like I remember one time, eh . . .' And Mammie would suck her teeth and say, 'Umm, now heself, he see spirit too.' But now they were laughing at me, so I tiptoed from the step for them not to see me out there and know that I had heard. It would make them laugh even more.
    My sister Cherish was six years old when she died, and for most of those six years I had only ever seen her leave the bed when our father carried her. Through Cherish, I came to know a side of my father that I never knew existed. Usually he was impatient with us children, my brother and me, and we were very quiet when he was around. He hardly ever spoke directly to us, except to quarrel about something, or to give an order.
    My mother said that from the time that Cherish was born, there was something special between the two of them. He looked at her lying next to my mother and chuckled deep inside his throat. His face crinkled up and he smiled. She said that she remembered him saying something like, 'Poor little thing,' not because he thought she was sick or anything, but as if just watching her there all small and defenceless-looking made him go all tender and loving. And to think that he had

wanted a boy!

My mother said that when Cherish was born, she was lighter-skinned than any of us had been. She was always very light-skinned compared to us, but Mammie said that was because she wasn't always out in the sunshine like we were. Daddy felt it was because she hadn't come to stay in this world, so that her face was always kind of transparent, as if you could almost see through it to the world that she had come from and was going to. My father was fanciful sometimes. My mother made a kind of sound in her throat and then said, 'Is only because the child was sick. That is all there is to it. Not enough sunshine.' Then after a while she said in a softer voice, 'But she wasn't for this world in truth, poor little thing.'

'Well,' said my aunt, 'if she wasn't for this world, she must be richer than us in fact.' She was silent for a while too, then she said, 'The Lord giveth and the Lord taketh away.'

'Amen,' my mother said.

My father grunted. Then after a while, as if he thought perhaps the Lord might be listening, he cleared his throat and said, 'Well, God knows best.'

My mother said that it was when Cherish was about three months old that she began to worry about her. When she held her up, the baby's head drooped to her shoulder, and she seemed to make no effort to lift it, like a baby normally would.

'Is like something wrong with her,' my mother said to my father. But he answered that perhaps she was just a bit slow, and everything would be all right.

After a while my mother began to worry more and she went with Cherish to the doctor. The doctor said not to worry too much. The head was a little heavy but she would grow it out. There was no need for concern. But Cherish's head kept on growing faster than her body. The body stayed thin and long and the head got bigger, and rounder, and almost transparent, and very soft. My mother cried often. And my father looked as if he wanted to cry, too, but really couldn't. They took Cherish to many different doctors. The doctors said they knew something was wrong, but couldn't say what. When Cherish was about eight months old, with a big round head and a long, thin, tiny body, one doctor said that she had water on the brain. My mother cried and prayed. Was there no cure for it? she wanted to know. No way of getting the water out? Was it something she had done while pregnant? Had the water got in because she was careless while bathing the child? The doctors said that she shouldn't blame herself, that it wasn't her fault, but they couldn't say whose fault it was.

And that was when my brother and I started to feel guilty. We had often been warned by our parents not to take the baby off the bed. At six and seven, they told us, we were too young to control the child's weight. We used to go often to watch her when she was in her cradle, lying there kicking her legs and laughing her toothless laugh at the ceiling. We liked best to watch her when it rained. As the rain pounded on the roof of the house, her tiny hands would go up, the right held slightly higher than the left; her right foot would be drawn close to her body, the left held higher and slightly more stretched, her fists tight as her eyes remained fixed on some spot beyond the range of our vision.

'She listening. She listening to the rain.'

'What happen, Cherish? You like it? You fraid?'

And as we touched her tiny fist to draw her attention, Cherish would laugh and move both feet and hands vigorously, laughing and laughing as if it were wonderful to be alive when it rained. She made us laugh, too, and when we were with her, my brother and I were always good friends. We found it most difficult to resist her when she lay on our parents' bed surrounded by pillows.

I don't remember what happened exactly, but I know that one day we tried to lift her. Perhaps we couldn't control her properly and her head drooped forward in a way it never did when our parents held her. Perhaps she cried. I don't remember. Yes, I think she started to cry and then when Mammie came running, me and Joseph said that we were just there watching her and playing with her and then she started to cry. And when Mammie asked if we had touched her or done something wicked like pinch her or anything, we said, 'No, Mammie, in truth, we were just there playing with her and then she started to cry.'

And then after that all I know is that when Mammie started to wonder if she might be responsible for Cherish's head being that size, my brother and I had the same thought about ourselves, remembering the one time that we had done the forbidden thing and lifted our sister off the bed. She didn't seem sick then. Suppose we had started it all by lifting her? Suppose we had knocked her head too hard when we put her down, so that the soft centre had started to expand? We only whispered to each other about it once and then were too afraid to talk with each other about it afterwards. We used to stand at our parents' bedside and watch her, looking at the big eyes in the long thin face, making her laugh and wondering if we were responsible. Joseph didn't say anything, but I knew that he was always thinking the same thing as me about that, especially because sometimes when we were standing near to her bed and I looked at him, he would frown and suck his teeth as if he was telling me to behave myself.

After Cherish died, whenever there was something on the news or in the newspaper about someone who had committed a murder, my brother and I would never have anything to say about if the person should be punished or not, and how. We would avoid each other's eyes and I know that we were both thinking about our terrible secret. I don't remember if we ever told our mother. I don't remember, but I know that in spite of everything I still feel guilty sometimes. That's why I know how my mother felt when she wondered if she was responsible.

After a while, our sister's head was so heavy that only our father could lift her right off the bed. And he did it with a tenderness that made us feel like crying.

'Cher? All right. Yes. Yes. You laughing, eh? A'right,

a'right! Oops! Daddy wouldn' hurt you, non. Eh, Cher? Ye-e-es! Good girl. Look how she laughin!'

We used to stand watching as Daddy lifted Cherish off the bed, helping him with our eyes, with our half-lifted hands, with our half-opened mouths, as if we would make it softer and easier for her just by watching. Cherish's small body would stiffen as he lifted her and her large eyes would wander to the roof and around the room, as if she was trying to figure out what was happening.

'You just going to the drawing-room to sit down for a while, eh? A'right? A'right, Cher?'

Her eyes would continue to look around vacantly, wondering, afraid, but still kind of secure because we were there. You ever see somebody eyes talk? Well it was just as if Cherish used to talk with her eyes. And I always used to think she felt kind of safe because we were there, especially after she had to leave us. At times, when there was no-one in the room with her she would really scream, and then get quiet when someone went in and sat by her bed.

Daddy often sat with her in the drawing-room. Sometimes she sat propped up in a specially-made chair that they had bought her. I don't remember if they bought it at the store, or if it was the carpenter down the road that they got to make it, but in any case they bought this kind of reclining chair for her. Occasionally Daddy carried her outside and we all sat watching her as she sat in the chair on the grass. Cherish loved this. She would roll her eyes trying to see the blue distance of the sky and the trees and she would laugh and laugh. Watching her, we laughed too, just smiled and showed our teeth watching Cherish laugh.

Our mother tried everything that she knew and found out about a lot that she didn't know. When the doctors agreed that it was water on the brain and that there was nothing we could do about it but watch and pray, we all prayed, but I think our mother prayed the hardest. She looked for God all around her and when she didn't find the answer she wanted, it was as if she went into every little corner looking for God.

'Sometimes you can't find the reason in things,' she said, 'is God alone that know.' She said this often, and each time she looked up at the sky, or at the roof if she was inside, and opened out her hands with the palms up.

'Lord, you self know I always say I baptise in the Anglican church and I have nowhere else to go to because is the same God that everywhere, but any church at all that could do something for this my child, Lord, I will follow them to the end of my days. Lord, if it be Thy will, Thy will be done. But please, Lord, cure my child.'

Miss Magdelene helped our mother to find one way to talk to God. Miss Magdelene started to come to us when Cherish was two years old. It was the year that our younger sister Hope was born. Now that I am talking about it, another thing that I remember is that my aunt Cleopatra didn't like that name, Hope.

'When for you to give the child a ordinary name like Mary or something, and make sure that she under the guidance of some saint, you calling her Hope. Is this new-fangled names and all these people that not thinking of the church that causing all the trouble. You was all right with the first two. Martha and Joseph is proper name. But with this last two I don't know what do you at all. How is Hope you go by now dey? And before that was Cherish. Who know if is that that do the child? What Cherish mean? Cherish!'

My mother was hurt. 'So you saying is me that responsible for how Cherish is today?'

'I not saying that. But who know how God does show his vexation?'

My mother didn't say anything for a while, which was unusual for her. And when I looked at her I could see that her eyes were full of tears. I looked at Auntie but she was watching something in the prayer book and her lips were moving and she didn't see the tears in my mother's eyes. Then all of a sudden Mammie got up and went outside to the kitchen for something. When she came back her eyes were dry and she said kind of quiet like, 'Is because of Cherish self I call this one Hope.'

My aunt didn't say anything and although I was afraid of God and wondered if he would do a thing like that in truth, I suddenly remembered hearing somebody say that she was not a real aunt, just someone my father's mother had taken to stay with them. And I was so vexed with her for doing that to our mother that I thought, that is why she could say that. Because Cherish not really related to her. Daddy wouldn't say that. Nobody else wouldn't say that. But then I thought it wasn't that alone, because I knew a lot of people not related to us who wouldn't say a thing like that and hurt my mother so. But after that I never felt good about my aunt. And I told my brother, and sometimes when nobody was around, we would tear a leaf out of my aunt's prayer book and leave it in there all rumpled. Or one day we hid her slippers. And sometimes when she called we just wouldn't answer. But the worst, worst thing we did and never admitted to was to push down the kind of wooden cross that used to hang on the door inside my aunt's room. We just meant for it to fall on the floor so that she would have to pick it up, but when it fell it broke and my brother and I had another secret that we couldn't tell anybody. And later on when my aunt was talking about the cross and saying that she didn't know how this cross could fall and break so, and that she thought she had felt the house shake a little bit during the day, so perhaps there had been a slight earthquake, we looked at the cross too and said, 'Oh, oh, but look what happen!'

My mother gave Hope two names. She called her Anne, so that she was christened Hope Anne Chandler. When all the rest of us called her Hope, my aunt Cleopatra always called her Anne.

But anyway, after Hope was born, Mammie was always tired. Cherish cried a lot in the night when she wet herself and couldn't turn or anything, or when she was tired of lying on one side and couldn't move herself. And now Hope started crying in the night too. So my mother was always getting up to see after both of them and in the morning she was really tired. My father got up once or twice, but he used to fret a lot, and sometimes after Cherish was crying for a long time, I would hear him through the partition from the room where me and my brother slept saying to my mother in the night, 'You don't hear the child crying, then?' Then my mother got up. Sometimes again she just sucked her teeth and said, 'You get up. Is you that could turn her properly.' And then my father would get up and go to Cherish. Then at times Hope woke up and started crying too.

In the morning my father would be muttering and saying, 'Well these children cry whole night, you know. I so tired, eh, they could well fire me from work today.' And he would leave in a really bad temper for his job driving the truck at the Public Works Department in St George's. And Mammie would be in a bad temper too if we didn't want to drink the cocoa or the soursop tea before we went to school.

Then one night after Cherish had really cried a lot, Daddy hired a car from town to come up and take her and Mammie to the doctor. It was a Saturday, when Daddy wasn't working, because by this time Mammie couldn't lift Cherish, and anyway the car couldn't drive right in. Daddy had to hold her up careful, careful and walk one today, one tomorrow, up the gap.

Auntie Cleopatra walked in front of him, backing back up the gap and saying, 'Put down you foot careful, now, it have a rough patch there,' and 'that is a big stone you puttin you foot on, eh, Joseph, and it kind of smooth. Go easy. Oops, watch it. Hold up, hold up. Go careful, now.'

And then when they had walked up the track to the road, Mammie was already sitting inside the car at the back so that she could help take some of the weight as Daddy sat down inside with Cherish, saying all the time, 'Cher, you all right? Um? Daddy wouldn't hurt you, non.'

Joseph and I stood with Auntie Cleopatra and watched them go, feeling as if it was a death or a real going away or something. The car drove off and Auntie Cleopatra said, 'You children go inside now. Go and find something to do.

Martha, make some tea for the other little one. You, Joseph, sweep up the leaves from the breadfruit tree that falling in the yard there. Come on, come on. Find something to do.' She walked up the steps saying, 'Trust in the Lord for all.'

The doctor said that it had reached a stage when he didn't think they could take care of Cherish at home like that. He said that with Hope young too, it was really too much and the whole house could have a breakdown if they continued like that; he thought it was best if they put her into the children's home in St George's. There were nurses there, he said, trained to do that, and it would take the pressure off the family.

When they came back home, our mother cried. And Daddy kept saying, 'Take it easy, non. So you want to start the family breakdown he talk about then? Take it easy, non.' He looked irritated and spoke kind of vexed-like to Mammie, sucking his teeth and everything, but later I saw him in the room kneeling next to Cher's bed and his face was hidden down on the bed, and I don't know if he was crying or just praying, but I got frightened and I didn't wait to see.

I asked my mother what the doctor meant when he said that the whole family could have a breakdown.

'He means it's too much for us,' my mother said.

'Yes, but he mean the *whole* family could . . . could . . .?'

My mother just said steupes, and turned away from me. I don't think I really believed that we could all go mad in the family because of Cherish, but I kept remembering that long-ago relative, and how bad it was to take on worries, and I began to be very nervous everytime she cried, and I would pray every night for her not to wake up and cry. And when she did, I woke up and stayed awake too until Mammie and Daddy settled down again. I listened to what they said, too, just to see if there were signs of a breakdown. It was after the visit to the doctor that Daddy talked about Miss Magdalene.

He came home one day, on a Saturday when he had to do some extra work, and said that his friend Vernon's mother, Magdalene, wouldn't mind having a little something to do that could bring in a few extra cents. It was one December, I remember, just before Christmas. Peas was in season and he was sitting there eating his pea soup. It was late, about half past five, and me and Joseph were sitting at the dining-table too doing our homework. Auntie Cleopatra and Auntie Genevieve, who were staying with us for a time because they were looking for work in the area, were sitting outside under the julie mango tree counting some story. I couldn't hear what they were saying but I remember that through the window I could see Auntie Genevieve's hand go up to her mouth and her eyes open wide. You could imagine that she was saying something like, 'Eh, my sister, you ever see a thing like that?' I was just about to touch Joe's knee under the table to get him to look out of the window and see her too so that we could laugh together when Daddy brought up the subject of Miss Magdalene, saying that she was looking for work helping out somebody. I remember it as clear as ever. You know how some things just stay in your mind? Mammie was sitting there nursing Hope. And she said, 'Um-hm. So what you thinking?'

Daddy said, 'Well,' in that way that sounded like, 'It should be kind of obvious what I'm thinking.' And he moved his hand as if to brush away the flies, only there weren't any flies around at the time. 'If we could manage to take her on, she could help you out in the house here, help a little bit in the garden around, taking care of the tomatoes and lettuce and things that getting so overgrown now, help you with the cooking sometimes, and to take care of the children. You know what I mean, anything that need doing.'

Mammie finished nursing Hope and put her up against her shoulder to burp. 'That would be a godsend,' she said. 'But where we going to get the money to pay her?'

Daddy put down his spoon and chewed on the peas, twisting his mouth to get at the really good bits.

'Hm. That is a question.' He looked outside to where Auntie Genevieve and Auntie Cleopatra were sitting. 'That is a question. But,' he took up the beef bone and started sucking at it, 'we have to try. Apparently,' he paused and cleared his throat, 'she wouldn't want what those big people and so could pay, you know; she would be satisfied with a small payment and whatever little peas and provision and tomatoes and so she could get from the garden here. Because as they living right in the heart of town there, those things expensive, so that would help out well.'

'Well yes,' said my mother, 'if she would agree to something that you think you could pay, and she would take whatever we could produce in the garden here, that sound good.'

'That is what I saying.' Daddy pushed back his chair a little bit, turned sideways and crossed his legs. 'And,' he put his head back and looked up at the rafters, the bone in his hand there waiting until he was ready, 'it going be an easy arrangement, you know; I talk to her already; she know how thing is, and she say that if one week things really bad, as long as we give her something to get by, she wouldn't make a fuss.'

'Well yes,' Mammie laughed, sounding excited. 'Well yes. That sound like it could be a godsend in truth.'

Daddy started sucking at the bone again and I giggled. Mammie looked at me cross-eyed, thinking that I was listening to big people conversation and laughing, but I was really laughing at the way Joseph was watching Daddy's bone and chewing with him. I knocked his knee under the table and he frowned at me, pulled his lips together and said, 'Girl, behave youself, non.'

Mammie stopped patting Hope's back for a moment and looked at the two of us and said, 'If you two can't behave, clear out!' Joseph muttered something and I stifled a giggle. He poked at my knee under the table and I would have knocked him down then and there, but I knew it would cause trouble, so I just waited to get at him later. Daddy put down the bone.

'I was thinking,' he said, 'that perhaps we could have asked Cleopatra, but . . .'

'Forget about that,' said Mammie. 'While she here and she could give a help, we thankful, but let her look for her work because we can't afford to pay her what she need to look after these dozen and one children that waiting on her to feed them.'

'Well, yes, that is what I been thinking.' He stretched his hands high above his head, letting the food go down. 'Hm! This Godfrey, eh! He don't even look back.'

'Well, forget bout he, because that is the livin dead. All the responsibility is on Cleopatra shoulders. And Genevieve self dey holdin on to this other one that you could take and tie a bundle of wood, he so lazy.'

Joseph and I giggled. Daddy chuckled. Mammie looked at us and said, 'The two of you siddown dey takin the words right out of me mouth, but leave it right where you hear it. I don't give you no message for nobody.'

'Ay! I doin my homework, yes.'

'Yes, because you homework is to stay with you bottom lip drooping and drink up every word I say. Clear out; go and make up a bed for Hope.'

'But, Mammie, I not finish . . .'

'Clear out, ka dammit, make up the bed and come back and finish you homework. You go and help her, Joey.'

'But Mammie . . .'

'Clear out, ka dammit.'

By the time we were finished with Hope's bed, the conversation was over. Miss Magdalene started coming to our house the Monday after that. She was really nice. She was old like, older than Mammie and Daddy and sort of like a grandmother, and really, really nice. She used to tell all sorts of stories, and lots of people in her family had seen spirits and things. And she loved Cherish. She would sit on a chair near to Cherish's bed and tell her all sorts of stories. And I'm sure Cherish understood. She laughed a lot, too, when the juicy parts of the story came along. And she would move her hands up and down, her eyes would roll around, and then she would be quiet again, just her eyes moving, and listening to

Magdie's voice.

It was Hope who started to call her Magdie when she couldn't say her name properly and was trying to say Magdalene. Sometimes we called her Magdie, too, but most times we just said Miss Magdalene – Mammie, Daddy, all of us. I remember one day Joseph stayed outside by under the mango tree and shout out, 'Magdalene!' I don't know what get into him. It was such a shock. I was in the kitchen with Mammie, and is just as if she didn't hear. She was there grating some coconut to boil oil, and humming a tune; she just raised her head a little bit and then bend down again over the grater and continue humming. I said to myself, if was me, she woulda turn me face wrongside with a box.

Mammie finish grating the piece of coconut and long, long after, she call quiet-like, 'Joseph!'

'Yes, Mammie.'

I don't know how Joseph didn't guess something, because from the time Mammie say, 'Joseph,' I thinking, 'Eh-heh! Something in the mortar besides the pestle.' But Joseph must have been real bazodee that day, because he come running from outside, making a sound with his mouth like a truck driving, and steering with his hands. He reach by the kitchen door, pull brakes, park the truck outside, and come inside.

'Yes, Mammie?'

Mammie was filling a cup with water from the pipe to pour it into the big bowl of coconut and she looked up at Joseph standing by the door, stopped the humming for a moment and said, 'Come.'

Perhaps Joseph thought it was to help her with the coconut or something, but he not usually so stupid; he went right up near to her, and she well take her time and catch him. She put down the cup in the sink, and turn around and hold his left hand hard. Is only then Joseph realise something wrong and he start to pull away. Is only then! Imagine that!

'Ay, Mammie, what happen?'

'Stop pulling, because you not stronger than me, Mister Man.' Mammie just stand up there looking at Joseph, and I don't believe she did mean to beat him. She just say, quiet-like, 'Now listen to me, and listen well.'

Joseph frowned. You could see the fear of a beating and the wonder about what wrong in his face, but me, right away I know. And I believe Joseph knew too, but he just pretending, because both of us know you can't speak to big people like that. But because Mammie take so long before she call him, he thought he did get away with it.

'Ay, Mammie.'

'Stop "Ay Mammie-ing" me, before I turn you face wrongside.'

I couldn't help it; I giggled, and then remembering myself, I put the towel that I was wiping the wares with to my face. Mammie watched me one cross-eye.

'The towel is for wiping the wares, not stuffing in you mouth.' I tried to disappear into the wall. I wanted her attention to stay with Joseph. She looked at him. 'So you and Miss Magdalene same age?' Joseph was silent.

'Answer me!'

'No, Mammie.'

'You is Miss Magdalene grandfather?'

'No, Mammie.'

'Somebody did call you to stand for her in church?'

I keep my face well straight, because I know that if I did so much as let it go, anything could happen. Joseph looked across at me under his eyes to see if I was laughing. But I just opened my eyes wide. I was standing too near to Mammie.

'I ask you a question, Joseph.'

'No, Mammie.'

'Well, gentleman! Next time I hear you calling her like a lord you will swallow you tongue, you hear me?'

'Yes, Mammie.'

'Miss Magdalene worth you grandmother. You ever hear me or you father shouting her out *Magdalene*, like a grand-master?'

'No, Mammie.'

'Well, watch yourself. And when you boots get too big to

fit inside here, build you own shack outside, you hear me?'

'Yes, Mammie.'

'Or else you will find that you might have to swallow me cuff whole.'

I had to bite the insides of my cheeks that time, otherwise I would surely have taken the licks for Joseph. And even so a kind of sound knocked at my throat. But Mammie didn't hear. She let Joseph go. But he really had the Devil with him that day, because before he could even reach by the kitchen door, he mutter, 'But ain't Miss Magdalene is a servant?'

Mammie moved so fast that the plate I was just picking up to wipe drop on the floor and mash up. Joseph didn't stand a chance to reach the door. She practically dragged him inside the house with her. Well at last Joseph sense return and he pulling away and bawling.

'I sorry, Mammie. I didn't mean that, Mammie. I know Miss Magdalene is not a servant, Mammie. Woy! Woy! Don't beat me, Mammie. I fraid licks, Mammie.'

By the time I clear up the big pieces of plate from the floor and reach inside by the drawing-room door, Mammie had Daddy's leather belt in her hand, and Joseph was dancing all around her. She lifted her hand.

'Woy!'

'Now Miss Magdalene is not your servant!'

'I know, Mammie!'

'Not today!'

'Don't beat me, Mammie. You don't have to beat me, Mammie. I know that, Mammie.'

'Not yesterday!'

'Yes, Mammie; yes, Mammie. I understand, Mammie.'

'Not anytime in the future!'

'Oh gosh, Mammie, it burnin, Mammie.'

'Leave him now, Miss Chandler. He didn't mean anything. He never rude with me. He just a little bit fresh, that is all. Leave him now.'

'Is the freshness I trying to get out of him. If he fresh he in the wrong place, because thing that fresh down in the sea.'

'Mammie I not fresh again, in truth, Mammie!'

'And if is so you think you have to talk about servants,' Mammie pulled Joseph from where he was wrapping himself behind her back, 'I hope you never have none.'

'Mammie, it hurtin in truth, Mammie.'

'Shut up! You smellin youself! Talking bout servant! Who is servant with you?'

Mammie let him go, and Joseph rushed to the door.

'Where you going? Come back and sit you tail right inside here, and understand that Miss Magdalene is a old woman with great-grandchildren older than you. Sit down there and think about that. And don't let me hear no noise from you.'

Joseph sobbed loudly.

'Swallow them! Swallow them, I say.' Mammie moved closer to him, and Joseph's sobs quietened. After Mammie went back to the kitchen, I went and sat near to him, but he pushed me away. For the rest of that day, Joseph was king. When Daddy came home, I heard him and Mammie talking quietly in the kitchen. Daddy chuckled.

'Well what happen to this child at all?'

'And I don't like to beat him, you know. But you think is licks self? He full up the house with bawling, but is you little thin belt I take and half of those lash fall on he clothes.'

'Eh-eh! So he want servant, yes?'

'Is like he feel he is man, you know.'

That night Mammie even called Joseph to help her in the kitchen, because she knew he liked to make saltfish souse. She let him cut up the tomatoes and onions and everything. And afterwards Mammie and Daddy talking about how the souse so nice. But it was just to make Joseph feel good, because the souse wasn't no nicer than usual. The whole time, though, Joseph only looked at the tablecloth. Even when Daddy leaned across and kind of laughed and touched him on the side of the head, he didn't say anything. Just pulled his head away and continue eating his souse.

Miss Magdalene stayed with us a long time. But then she started to get tired too, and she couldn't be there all the time.

She helped Mammie a lot with Cherish, though, and you could see that Cherish liked her. Things were getting really difficult after a time, because Cherish was getting big and by the time she was five years old, the head was so big that Daddy couldn't even lift her from the bed comfortable again. He could do it in a way, but it was very awkward for him. And Cherish started getting sores, too. Mammie said that those on her bottom were because she was always wetting herself and we had to keep turning her.

Sometimes she would be crying so much that Mammie would say, 'But, sweetheart, I can't turn you anywhere else; is only two sides you have, and I just turn you from the other one. Okay, love? All right?' But Cherish would go right on crying, because she was hurting. You see, she couldn't eat any solid food, so she was always drinking milk and water and juice and things like that, and sometimes before she well finish drinking, it would come right back out again.

When I think about it now, I feel really bad, because in the afternoon, after Miss Magdalene went home, when we had come back from school, we would pretend not to hear Mammie when she was calling us to help with Cherish. Sometimes we would be sitting right there on the step, and as soon as Cherish started to cry, we would sneak away, because Mammie might be preparing something for Hope, and we knew that she was going to call us. So we would run far away where she couldn't find us. And at times Hope would see us running and tell Mammie. But then she stopped, because after she did that, we wouldn't let her play with us at all for a long time. Hope was a real little newsmonger that time. She's still like that sometimes, but she's a little better now that she's getting older. She was almost four when Cherish died, and she will soon be five, so she has more sense now.

But anyway, with all the sores on her body, Cherish was crying a lot night and day. And Mammie and Daddy were always arguing. And sometimes it was Miss Magdalene that had to part them.

Once, when Cherish started getting sores on her head, they

called the doctor to come and see her. He said it was because of the water inside, and because the head needed to be turned often, too, but it was so heavy. And besides, sometimes when Daddy was turning it, it was as if it hurt her, so she would cry. And once after Daddy turned her, I believe he hurt her neck, and she screamed so much that Daddy sat there next to her and started to cry. And Mammie went and touched him and said, 'Is all right, is not your fault, Joe.' Joseph had the same name as our father, and when Mammie talked like this it sounded as if it wasn't Joseph my father but Joseph my brother she was talking to. But it was really our father, because he was so sad for Cherish. 'Is not your fault, Joe. You couldn't help it. Is because the head heavy. Is not your fault.'

And sometimes both of them would turn her together, or me and Mammie would turn her. Mammie would put her hands under the head on one side, turn it, and then tell me to ease the other side a little bit, and together we would turn her on the other side. Sometimes Mammie and Joseph would turn her, or sometimes Mammie and Miss Magdalene, but Joseph and I never turned her together or alone. And whenever someone was turning her, Hope would stand a little way off with her head to one side and say, 'Oh, oh! Careful, now! Careful!' She was really nice sometimes, only that she was such a little newsmonger.

Hope liked to sit down and talk to Cherish. Sometimes, she would take a book, push a chair near to the bed, climb up and sit there and pretend to read to her, saying things like

> One little piggy went to market
> And one little piggy stayed home
> And one little piggy had roasted beef
> And one little piggy had none.

When she couldn't say it properly, it sounded like 'Awn ittu piddy ent to martet, and awn ittu piddy stayed ome.' We would walk into the room and the two of them would be there laughing away. But one day after Cherish screamed out,

Mammie said she believed that Hope had pinched her, because we had seen her do it once. And that day when Mammie went in after the scream, she was just standing there with the end of her dress in her mouth, sucking it and looking at Cherish without saying anything. So after that, we closed the door so that Hope couldn't go in there alone until she was old enough to understand that she shouldn't pinch her.

We used to leave the windows wide open in Mammie and Daddy's room, where Cherish used to be, and tie up the curtains, so that she could see the trees all of the time. She liked that. When the wind blew a little bit and the trees rustled, she laughed out loud and made sounds in her throat; it was almost as if she was talking to the wind. Sometimes when we went into the room she would be there just looking at the open window and laughing. Then she would be quiet and listening, and start laughing all of a sudden, as though someone else had said something to amuse here.

Once Mammie and I went in together and stood up watching her. While she was listening, I said, 'Cher?' and she jumped and started to cry.

Mammie said, 'Sh-h-h! Don't interrupt her like that! Sh-h! All right, Cher!' And Mammie just put the net over her, because we used to cover her with a net sometimes, especially during fly season; then she put her finger to her mouth to make me keep quiet, and motioned me towards the door.

'How you mean don't interrupt her, Mammie?'

'She was conversing.'

'Conversing? With who?'

'With people that we can't see. She in another world.'

'Um.' I was annoyed.

My mother laughed. She knew that I got annoyed about things that I couldn't understand but which scared me a little.

'You frightened?'

I sucked my teeth. 'You self always saying it don't have spirits.'

'There are more things in heaven and earth than we could understand.'

I was not satisfied, but my mother started humming, and I couldn't think of a suitable question to interrupt her with. Not one that would make her stop humming. But sometimes I think that this is partly why I felt that way when I saw the bird.

One night, after Hope was ill, and Cherish was crying, and none of us slept much for the night, Miss Magdalene told our mother that she should buy a candle and give to her to put on the altar in the Catholic church.

They were talking just outside the kitchen door, the place where I always imagined a truck was parked, because that day after Joseph got his beating, he never went back for the truck he had parked there. Anyway, they stood there talking and I remained very quiet in the kitchen, because I knew that if Mammie remembered I was there, she would move away, or motion to Miss Magdalene to leave the conversation for later.

'Buy a candle?' my mother asked.

'Yes, things getting really bad now with the little one, and it wearing you out, so you have to ask for the Lord's help, child.'

'I praying night and day. God self know I always bend me knee in prayer for that little girl. I even send off to *Daily Word* to get people to pray in fellowship with me.'

'That good. That good, Miss Chandler. But prayers never too much. And in the Catholic church, the prayers there good, good. Dem is the best. They prayers really strong. Barring going and see those other people that you say you don't like to go to there, dem is the best.'

'You not talking about . . .' my mother paused and I thought perhaps she had remembered me, so I tiptoed and stooped down behind the big barrel where we collected water for in case there was none in the pipe. I don't know if she peeped inside of the kitchen, but as I strained to hear from behind the barrel, I heard her say in a low, low voice, 'You mean like obeah, Miss Magdalene?'

'No, no,' said Miss Magdalene. 'I not talking about anything like that at all. A lot of the big, big people who does go to church every day does put a candle in front of the saints to ask for a special favour sometimes. Is the same thing.'

'But . . .'

'Is the same thing, I telling you, Miss Chandler. Is nothing to fraid. Is the same thing that people does do from time. They say is a good thing to put a candle in front of St Anne, especially, and to say a prayer for whatever it is you want. And a really good thing to do, besides putting a candle in the side-aisle by where St Anne does be, is to give another candle to the priest special, so that he could put it on the altar during the mass, and ask him to offer up special prayers for a something private for you. You don' even have to say what.'

'Well, yes, I will try that. Anything that could help, Miss Magdelene. Anything at all, yes, with this child that on me hand dey.'

'All right then! If you give me two candles end of the week, I will bring them in the church for you.'

'Okay. I will take it in the message from the shop this week.'

I tiptoed from behind the barrel after that, and went inside, so I don't know what else went on, but I was really excited. It was a good secret. I didn't even tell Joseph, because it felt so important, having to do with God and everything. The candle must have gone in to the church that Sunday, and believe me eh, for the whole of the next week, Cherish was really quiet, laughing all the time, and we could sleep in peace. I even heard Daddy commenting about how she improve. I hear Mammie saying is a miracle, but I don't know if she told him that it was a miracle in truth, because although I listened a lot to what they were saying, I never heard anything. They probably said it when I wasn't around. Because Mammie was always looking at me as if she felt I listened to her conversations, and one day she even asked me if I wanted to rent a spot inside of her mouth. It was at the dining-table, and all of the others laughed, even Hope, and Joseph too, although I cut my eyes at him.

And Daddy looked at me as if he thought I deserved that.

And he said, 'I hope you give as much attention to your school-work.'

So I said, 'I don't want spot inside nobody mouth!'

'What is that?'

'Nothing, Daddy!'

'It better be nothing!'

I tried to talk to Miss Magdalene about the church, too, but she just looked at me and said, 'I see why Miss Chandler does say that the walls in this house have long ears!'

After that good week, Cherish started to get sores and cry again. I wanted to advise Mammie to try the candle again, but I didn't have the courage. I don't know if she ever tried it another time, but Cherish kept getting worse and crying more.

Once, some preachers came to Grenada. Everybody said that they were very good. They were preachers from the United States of America, Born Again Christians, and they were good. They called on the Lord and did healing; the talk was that lots of people who were very ill had been healed. They even said that one woman who hadn't walked for years threw away her chair when the preacher prayed and laid his hands upon her. Auntie Genevieve said that she leapt to her feet, threw away her chair, and walked, testifying that she was healed. 'God be praised,' said Auntie Genevieve.

'You know, I going to that meeting tent in Queen's Park, yes,' my mother said one day.

'For truth?' Our aunt – Auntie Cleopatra, that is, because she was the one who was usually with us – she sounded surprised. 'You would go there?'

'Go, yes.' Miss Magdalene was certain. 'Go, Miss Chandler. I telling you, eh, anything that could work, anything at all, at all, try it, yes! Perhaps is only a miracle that could cure her. Who know what wrong with the child? An we shouldn' take away she chances. Go, you hear, Ma. And they say the man good, you know. Pastor Johnson. They say when you see he cast out the spirits so, the people just jumpin' on the stage and shouting for joy!'

'Well, nobody will shout for joy more than me if he make Cherish walk! This is one time the world will hear me testify!'

'You right, yes. Go an see what he could do for you!'

Our mother went. Daddy went, too. He and his friend, Miss Magdalene's son, were carrying Cherish on a kind of stretcher like, and walking slow. Mammie said that she walked right to the front of that huge crowd and they sat with Cherish in the front row. Cherish was almost five years old at that time. Whatever goodness was there, Mammie wanted our Cherish to get all of it. Pastor Johnson prayed. Pastor Johnson prayed for the entire congregation. Mammie shouted, 'Amen dear Jesus,' as loudly as anybody else, and placed her right hand on Cherish's head, all the while watching her face. I didn't go with them, but Miss Magdalene went, and she told me all about it afterwards. Mammie looked at Pastor Johnson's face. He prayed. He asked for those who wanted special prayers and Mammie's hand went up before anybody else could put up their hand. Pastor Johnson walked to the front row, and Miss Magdalene said he asked, 'Sister, the prayers are for this little one here?'

And Mammie said, 'Yes, Pastor.'

And then the Pastor asked, 'What seems to be the matter, sister?'

And Miss Magdalene said it was really funny, because Mammie said something like, 'The head is growing, Doc . . . er, Pastor.'

And Pastor Johnson took the mistake right up, and he kind of smiled and said, 'You're right, my sister. I am God's chosen doctor. Do you believe?'

Miss Magdalene is something else. When she telling me and Joseph the story, she say, 'Look eh, the pastor so good he say, "Doctor, priest, whatever you want to give me, me is that." '

And afterwards we heard Mammie telling Daddy that when the pastor asked about believing, she wanted to ask him, 'What? Believe what? That you are God's chosen doctor, or that my child would be healed? To tell you the truth,' said Mammie, 'I couldn't care less whether he think he is God's chosen doctor or the Devil incarnate, but at that moment if is belief that could heal my child, how ah don' believe dey! Nobody inside there believe more than me. I believe anything they want me to believe.'

And so she said, 'Yes, Pastor, I believe.'

Pastor Johnson held up his hand high and Miss Magdalene really jokey yes. She say that he almost go to meet his maker; he was stretching up so much on his toes. He punched the air with his fist and shouted 'Praise the Lord,' and all of them kept watching Cherish's face to see if any change was happening.

And Pastor Johnson asked Mammie, 'What is your name, sister?'

'Marybelle.'

'And the little one?'

'Cherish.'

'Oh yes, my sister. She is God's cherished one, too.' All of them who went, Miss Magdalene, Mammie and Daddy, said that just that made them feel better about the preacher.

But Miss Magdalene was the best one. I wish I could tell you the story and act it out like her. She told us the whole preacher's prayer, and when Joseph asked, 'Is so he say it?' she stopped and said it slow like, in a deep voice, not to mock, you understand, but because she could see we wanted to get the feel of everything that happened. And although I'm not sure I remember it exactly, Magdie's prayer from the preacher went something like, 'Oh Lord our God, look down upon this your servant Cherish. Suffer this child of your suffering, this child for whom you gave your pure and gentle life, to come right to you in health and beauty, Lord.'

And then the congregation said, 'True, Lord. Amen, dear Jesus. Isn't it true, Lord! You self see, Lord! Oh, yes!' And Mammie, too, was saying things like, 'Yes, Lord; we will serve you always, Lord.'

Well, Miss Magdalene said so, and knowing how much Mammie wanted Cherish to be cured, I know it's true, but I really can't picture it. Not Mammie. It just goes to show. Miss Magdalene said that Daddy sat next to her looking at Cherish's face, too, screwing his lips to one side and occasionally clearing his throat. We know that this is true, because Daddy often looks like that when he is thinking hard. And Magdie said that sometimes he leaned forward a little to peep into Cherish's face, just to see what was happening. Miss Magdalene didn't tell us what she herself said, but I could imagine she must have been muttering prayers, too. Because she loved Cherish. Even me would have mutter some deep prayers if I was there.

And then when Pastor Johnson rested his hand on Cherish's head, Magdie said that our sister's body stiffened. Her eyes moved quickly around like she was wondering what was happening. And the little hands stretched out stiff and straight in front of her. Cherish began to fret. Cranking up to cry, as Mammie would say.

And then our Dad got all soft and tender, running his fingers along the top of her head. Magdie said that he was saying, gentle like, 'All right, eh, Cher. Is nothing. Is all right.' And Cherish kind of relaxed a little bit. And Daddy said, 'Cher?' and leaned over, so that she could see his face. And Cherish acutally opened her mouth and laughed out loud. 'That child really like the father, you know,' Magdie said.

The pastor prayed some more. Magdie said that he talked about the leper woman and the hem of Jesus's garment. This was very sad, because it sounded like church, and Magdie lowered her voice when she got to this part, and we were very quiet. And the preacher prayed his main prayer, and I'm almost sure I remember it exactly as Magdie said it. 'Lord, let your healing come through my fingers. You who healed the leper woman when she touched but the hem of your garment, heal, I say heal! I say heal this your innocent servant, Lord. Let your healing truth pass through my fingers onto the suffering spot. In the name of God who can cast away devils, *be healed*!' And the congregation moaned and chanted. 'Oh

Jesus!' And through the whole prayer Cherish's eyes were searching Daddy's face. And then at the end of the prayer, when the pastor's voice stopped, she laughed again.

Magdie said that the pastor was sweating by the time he was finished. And he told Mammie that she should watch Cherish for a few days and see the Lord's healing work. I didn't hear Daddy saying how he felt, but I heard Mammie telling him that she tried hard the whole time not to listen to the doubting Thomas from the Bible. I know that our mother really wanted to believe, because she was baptised that day. She showed us the certificate when she came home. It was printed in Tennessee, USA. Towards the top part of the certificate was a drawing of the kind of scene that in my schoolbook was called lush green valleys, on either side of a meandering stream of blue water. I remember that word well, 'meandering', because Miss made us spell it once. It had little light blue markings at the top of the scene, like a sky that was coming and going. Then right around the edge of the certificate was a kind of green criss-cross line like a chain around the words. The words at the bottom of the lush green valleys said:

Baptismal Certificate

This certifies that
In obedience to the command and in imitation of the
example of our Lord Jesus Christ
Marybelle Chandler

was 'buried with Him in baptism' on the
<u>*1st*</u> day of <u>*August 1960*</u>
at <u>*St George's Grenada*</u>.

Our mother left the certificate on the dressing table. For days we would go to stand looking at it, my brother and I, thinking of a new mother buried with the Lord in baptism. Then we would look at Cherish lying on the bed, her eyes circling the room, her mouth opening into a welcome smile if we went closer. We would stand there and push our finger into her tightened fist. Cherish would move her hands and make sounds of pleasure. And my brother and I would laugh and watch the head closely to see if it was getting any smaller.

One day I saw our mother standing and watching the head, too. One day she said she thought it looked as if the growing had stopped. We were sitting at the table eating then and my father grunted, but he didn't say anything.

'Ah well,' my mother said, 'thy will be done.'

And then one day, I don't remember how long it was after the healing at Queen's Park, the certificate disappeared from the top of the dressing table. And my mother never talked again about the healing.

And then some time afterwards Miss Magdalene started having really bad arthritis, and for weeks she didn't come to our house. Both Auntie Genevieve and Auntie Cleopatra were working, too, and we hardly saw them. And most of Mammie's relatives were living far up in the country, and working too, so that that they didn't visit us much. And then one day Joseph surprised me. We were sitting under the mango tree. It was drizzling kind of light, but the sun was shining really hot, so the Devil and his wife must have been fighting like hell. Anyway, we were sitting outside there, and hoping no-one would look outside and tell us to get out of the rain.

'Mammie don't have time to think about us,' said Joseph, 'she wondering if is to put Cherish in a hospital.'

'What *sut* you talking, boy?'

'You always know who talking *sut*.'

'But why you say that?'

'I talking *sut*.'

He wouldn't tell me now. And if I tried to fight him, it would be worse. I sucked my teeth and yawned. I looked up at the branches of the mango tree. A leaf fell. I stretched out my hand so that it would touch me as it fell. It did. I was really pleased.

'The leaf fall on me, yes. I getting a letter, boy.'

Joseph sucked his teeth. I stood up and stretched. 'Like the drizzle getting stronger. I better go inside.' Joseph stopped whittling at the mango stick and looked up at me.

'I hear Mammie and Daddy talking this afternoon when you went to tie the sheep under the house. When they went in town yesterday, they went to see the children's hospital Mammie say the children well taken care of, and perhaps it's best to put Cherish there.'

'But they can't do that. How they could do that to Cherish?'

'Well somebody have to look after her, you know. And now that Mammie pregnant again . . .'

'Never!'

'Don't talk loud so, girl!' We both looked towards the house, but it seemed that no-one had heard us. I stared at Joseph. 'Is Daddy I hear saying that while they talkin' today. Mammie pregnant, Miss Magdalene sick, Hope still small, and it just too much for Mammie.'

'But I didn't know Mom . . .'

'Since when you calling her Mom? Nowadays I only hearing you with this Mom, Mom. Since when?'

I didn't say anything. It was because some of the girls at school said Mummy, but that sounded too strange in my mouth, so I kind of dragged the Mammie into a sort of half-Mummy, and so sometimes I said Mommy or Mom. I wasn't going to explain that to Joseph, because I knew he would just look at me with scorn and suck his teeth. Joseph was like that sometimes. He didn't like to change things. So I just sucked my teeth.

'Well, Mammie, then. I . . . well, I just don't know what to say.'

'I bet you they tell us that they will do that. Watch you gon see.'

They told us about two days later, when we came home

from school. And they took us to see the hospital. The children looked clean and nice. Two of them didn't have anything wrong with them. Just that there was no-one to take care of them. This was strange, because there was always someone to take care of children, some relative somewhere, but these two little children didn't have anyone who wanted them. But they looked happy in the hospital, talking and laughing to the nurses, and helping to carry things. They were twins, about five or six years old, and they came to talk to us. They asked us if we wee coming to live there too. Joseph and I just shook our heads. There were children who couldn't talk, too. And a little boy with no hands. But there wasn't anyone like Cherish there.

'You sure she will be all right, Mammie?'

'Yes. Two nurses came to see her yesterday, while youall were at school. They say she will be all right.'

Joseph and I didn't say anything. But perhaps Mammie could see that we wanted to cry.

'You children understand that Cherish getting too much for me? That I really can't take care of her at home anymore?' Mammie sounded as if she wanted to cry, too.

Then Daddy said, 'Cherish getting too much for your mother. She can't manage anymore on her own. You understand?'

'Yes, Daddy.'

Cherish went to the hospital in September. I don't remember what time in September, exactly. But I remember that it was September. Joseph and I went to see her three times, because we had to wait until Mammie or Daddy took the bus and went with us. Both of them went all the time, but Mammie went sometimes while we were at school.

What Joseph had said was true too. I only knew because one day a lady up the road asked me if I was glad that I was going to get a new little sister or brother. Fancy that! I don't know how I felt, just kind of strange, and I didn't even tell Joseph, or Mammie, and not Daddy of course. Daddy went sometimes to see Cherish during his lunch-break when he went to work.

The last time I went to see Cherish it was some time in October. She had sores, still, and her bed was wet, and she was crying. Mammie said she wasn't always like that. She reminded me that Cherish used to be like that at home sometimes, and said it didn't mean that they weren't taking care of her at the hospital. I remember Joseph started crying. He was just standing there and clenching his teeth and a sobbing sound was coming from his throat.

I tried to stop him, saying 'Is all right, Joseph. She not seeing trouble.' I put my arm around his shoulder, and he just continued sobbing quietly, looking at Cherish and crying. 'Joseph, if you don't stop that, Mammie will start crying, too, you know. And you know you don't want that to happen.' But I was crying too, now, and I couldn't help it, and when I looked at Mammie her lips were trembling. And Daddy just turned and walked out of the room. And then Mammie changed Cherish. We stayed with her a while. Daddy came back into the room afterwards, and by the time we left it was a little better, because Cherish was laughing.

When we were going home on the bus, Joseph asked Mammie if children couldn't go and stay for a night, sometimes. Mammie said it was a good idea, and she would ask the nurse, so that when we got holiday from school, we could probably stay a night sometimes. I was proud of Joseph. I looked at him different after that, like a person with sense. I thought it was such a good idea. But it never happened.

One morning early, about six o'clock, a little boy came running into the yard while I was brushing my teeth to get ready for school. He came with a message from the man in the shop out the road. The hospital had telephoned them to ask them to get a message to us. Cherish was dead. She had died in her sleep the night before. Mammie and Daddy left right away for the hospital and we didn't go to school that day.

Mammie said afterwards that she didn't want to tell us children anything, but she could see Cherish slipping away. *I* hadn't wanted to say anything, but I had noticed something strange, too. Because the last time we visited, Cherish's eyes didn't look secure any more when we touched her, or when we made her laugh, or when they were just wandering around the room. I think that is why I cried so much. Because I could see that she missed us, and missed the window through which she could see the trees, and missed hearing Daddy's voice all the time, and missed us touching her.

Mammie said that Cherish was happier now. And in a way I believed her. The day that Cherish died, I went into the room and looked at the bed where she used to lie down before, and I said 'Cherish. You all right, eh?' And I just felt that she was all right. And in a way I felt as if she was back with us again, and that was better than being in the hospital. Joseph looked at the bed, too. I know that he cried, but I think he felt better, too. All of us cried at home, quiet-like. I mean I saw everybody crying, except Daddy. I know for certain sure that he cry too, because of the way he was with Cherish, but when we were crying, he just blinked a lot, and cleared his throat, and then he walk away. Perhaps that is when he cried, when he went into the bathroom.

And Miss Magdalene came home and she cried, too. And Mammie's relatives came, and Auntie Genevieve and Auntie Cleopatra came. And Mammie's sisters, two in Brooklyn and one in London, sent telegrams. And Aunt Cleopatra said, 'The Lord giveth and the Lord taketh away.' And Auntie Magdalene said, 'Yes, this one is his angel for sure. Never did a bad thing in her life.' Daddy said, 'She wasn't for this world. I never see a prettier child.'

None of us cried at the funeral. You could see people looking at us and wondering why we didn't cry, and thinking perhaps that we didn't care about Cherish. But in a way I think we were all happy that she wasn't suffering now, and that she was back with us at home again. At least that is how I felt. The organ played for the funeral, and Mammie said that was really good, the choir members turn out well, because is not all funerals they play the organ for. It was beautiful. And the choir sang 'Suffer the little Children to Come Unto Me'.

When I saw the bird that morning, I remembered all of that, so it must have been like the day after the funeral, and the funeral was two days after Cherish died. And you know, I believe that Cherish is somewhere; I believe that she is listening to all of this. And I'd better stop this story, because I've told you the main things that I wanted to say, how we loved Cherish, and that she is happy now. And I'm always afraid of thinking about things like spirits and so, but Mammie is right, if Cherish *is* really a spirit, then she is a good spirit, but still, I don't want to see her, because I can't handle the idea of seeing any spirit, good or bad. So let me cross my fingers and stop this story.

And make the sign of the cross.